# Salvager

Lauren "Joe" Welch

© 2017 Lauren "Joe" Welch
All rights reserved.

ISBN: 1546649832
ISBN 13: 9781546649830
Library of Congress Control Number: 2017907947
CreateSpace Independent Publishing Platform
North Charleston, South Carolina
Back cover sketch of author by artist Dorian McGowan

# 1

MY MECHANIC FRIEND shook his head. A frown gave away his opinion: Someone wanted me to have an accident.

"No, I can't say beyond the shadow of a doubt, Mark." He held out one of the parts, a rusted, pitted fitting with a short stub of tubing protruding from one end. "See this place here, where it screws into the caliper. A lot of corrosion all around and rust. Same on the other one. But this little crack where it leaked? See how it's all shiny? Looks to me like the line was purposely bent. Just slightly. But enough to open it up with any pressure. Same thing on that one."

I studied the part he was holding, then more closely as he handed it to me. I felt around the area of the crack.

"So..." Looking at him, I didn't know where I was going with it.

He shrugged. "Hey, it's possible they both let go at the same time on their own. Possible, but I'd say damned unlikely. Especially diagonal wheels. Killed the whole system."

"And almost me."

We were talking about the failed brakes on my eleven-year old Toyota pickup truck. The morning before I'd narrowly avoided what could have been a fatal accident at the intersection below the steep hill leading down from the apartment building I called home.

A lesser man than Lenny might have turned it into a sermon, reminding me of my chronic negligence in maintaining the emergency brake; recalling the trouble he'd had each year repairing it to comply with the State of Vermont's inspection standards. Instead, he said, "Here. Let me get a bag. You need to take 'em with you."

"As evidence?" I laughed, but half-heartedly.

"Seriously. Know anybody who'd have it in for you?"

"None who'd go this far."

That was the beginning of it all, at least the first indication I had of someone's homicidal intent toward me; only upon later reflection and with a newly developed sense of suspicion would I recognize that an earlier incident had also been a likely attempt on my life.

I'd been honest in answering Lenny. At that moment in his garage I couldn't think of anyone who'd have it in for me enough to bother tampering with my brakes. If it had happened two years earlier I'd have put Ellen, my then estranged—now ex-wife at the top of the list. Not Ellen herself but a hit man. The heat of her wrath had cooled, however, most notably after her victory in court when the female judge had awarded her full custody of our two kids. During the year and a half since, except for an occasional screw-up over the visitation schedule, there'd been no further creative acts of spite. I suppose the joy from receiving a monthly child support check outweighed the kicks she got from harassing me. At any rate, I was the gift that would keep on giving but only if I, Mark Sloan, were alive to give.

Two other people did come to mind briefly, not at Lenny's but afterward, when I'd given it more thought. Namely two brothers, Roger and Little Don (or "Donny") Dornier. I'd locked horns in arguments with one and was currently researching connections the other had with a local development project. I disliked them and each had made it clear the feeling was mutual. At that point, however, I couldn't see a sufficient basis for either one taking such drastic action against me. In addition, even entertaining the thought of a Dornier family member being bent on murder seemed blasphemous.

In Collinsville the Dorniers were a protected species. Accuse any member of the clan of anything and you'd better back it up with rock solid evidence.

Lenny's little brown paper bag fitted neatly between lamp and toaster on my dilapidated kitchen table cum writing desk. Another knick-knack consistent with the decor, contributing to the over-all ambience of squalor. Like the cramped and rundown two-room apartment itself, the bag provided yet another symbol of my failure. First, the loss of a family and home. Then the loss of a full-time job. Now, in a brown paper bag, tangible evidence that someone wanted to kill me. These sorts of things only happened to losers. During the next few days, between bouts of self-loathing, I pondered over who might have tampered with my brakes. Neither the self-loathing nor the speculation proved especially productive.

I am a carpenter by trade. A thoroughgoing Carhartt's man. (Carhartts are those work jackets and pants made of a heavy-duty, canvas-like material, the pants doubled in thickness from the front pockets down to below the knees, equipped with handy, sewn-in loops below the belt-line made for hanging a hammer. Mine are mostly tan colored.) I love the feel of hand tools that measure, that cut, that drive nails and screws, that plane phyllo-like curls of wood. I love the scent of wood while shaping it, while sanding it; I love its texture and grain. I love the warm satisfaction from forming it to specification and stepping back and admiring the end product. I love creating and my medium is wood.

Being a carpenter wasn't at all what my parents, both educators, had likely hoped I would become when they footed the bill for my first year at a state college in Northeastern Vermont. They had assid-uously avoided pushing me in any specific vocational direction but I'm sure the pitiful muck-up my older sister, Charlotte, was making of her life at that time weighed heavily on them, heightening their anxiety over any aspirations they had for me.

I did well enough, but the following fall, having enjoyed a summer job with a small local building contractor in the nearby town of Collinsville, I decided against re-enrolling as a sophomore and instead accepted the contractor's offer of full-time, permanent employment.

My parents received the news with commendable equanimity, both of them, I knew, assuming I'd come to my senses when the novelty of the hard labor wore off. That didn't happen. I'd worked either full or part-time for Todd Drake, Building Contractor, ever since, going on seventeen years. Only my father had ever alluded to their disappointment, mildly at my last visit to him in the hospital about a week before he died of cancer. He'd quickly followed it up with a comment to the effect that it was more important to be happy in life and that I appeared to be happy doing what I was doing. (Luckily, this had preceded my estrangement from Ellen by about three years.)

Although I'd become fairly good at carpentry, both rough and finish, like so many workers scratching out a living in the Northeast corner of Vermont (often referred to as the Northeast Kingdom) I'd been forced to...well, diversify. The previous winter, about nine months before the failed-brake incident, Todd had needed to cut my hours drastically due to the dramatic downturn in construction brought on by the recession. He'd barely scraped together enough work to keep himself—along with his son, starting in June—busy, but on most of the jobs he'd managed to give me twenty-five, sometimes thirty hours a week. I'd filed for unemployment benefits to supplement my income, although many weeks it wasn't worth the hassle of computing irregular weekly earnings and dealing with the state's automated phone claim system. Basically, I wanted to work. It was early during that lean period when I took up what might seem an unlikely second occupation: newspaper reporting.

Ellen, my ex, may have it right. I probably am the nasty, degenerate, good-for-nothing bastard she claims. No one, however, not even golden-haired Ellen has ever credibly applied the epithet "lazy" to describe me. Maybe they haven't done that because to an extent I've succeeded in emulating the people I've always admired the most, the ones who refuse to let adversity win. Who stare it down. Who use every ounce of courage and determination to overcome it. Financial hardship in particular brings out the best in these people, their creativity, their sweat, their finest effort. They are quite the opposite of lazy. By their resourcefulness they become landscapers when roofing jobs dry up. The next year, unable to compete in an environment overabundant with landscapers, they become carpenters or loggers, or get hired as road construction workers. Through necessity they learn each role fast because they must to survive.

My friend Albert Fortin is one of these people. Big Al is the quintessential survivor. He rarely talks about the challenges he's overcome in life—a typical characteristic of the breed—but I know for a fact they include three bouts with cancer and two failed marriages. (A reputable source told me one of Al's exes, put alongside mine, would have made Ellen a winning candidate against any Miss Congeniality ever crowned.) Al smokes, drinks a lot of coffee and attends a meeting every Saturday night in the basement of the Collinsville Congregational Church. A few years ago he was also let go from what he'll describe as an extremely lucrative job. Whatever the circumstances were he believed he'd either need to move from Collinsville, the source of his roots, or get into some other line of work to support himself.

Al must have been around sixty then, too early for Social Security. He likes variety in what he does and of course, independence, which pointed toward self-employment. Al has opinions, strong opinions on about every subject there is. But unlike the majority of opinionated people, he takes the time to study all sides of every issue before reaching a judgment. He's never been one to hide his opinions either, to shrink from expressing them if they're controversial or run counter to what most other people think.

When it happened, no one who knew Al Fortin well should have been surprised to learn that he'd bought out the Collinsville Banner, a tiny weekly newspaper, then little more than a six to ten page shoppers guide with a few local news items, gossip, and photos thrown in.

"Mac had the right idea," he told me, "just lacked the balls to take a stand. Lots of pictures, especially of kids. Get all the names. Spell them correctly in the captions. That's the secret. Old Mac got it mostly right except he couldn't always call a spade a spade." Frederick McDougall, alias Mac, had parted with the paper for a "pittance," according to Al, he guessed because Mac was in his late-seventies by then and had lost the energy and interest to keep it going.

During the six-plus years he'd owned the paper, Al had hustled. It showed. A casual observer might doubt anything newsworthy can happen week in and week out in a village the size of Collinsville, population 5,300, but Al knew otherwise and proved it. He expanded his base of advertisers, extended his news coverage, printed more in-depth articles exploring village issues as well as state-wide issues having local relevance. He included at least one interesting feature story in each issue and also created an editorial page on which to personally sound off and to allow readers to in a letters section.

At the end of the third week in a row that Todd had been forced to cut my hours, I told him I needed to apply for other part-time work. I mentioned a couple of places I might apply and then, more in jest than anything I said, "Hell, maybe I'll talk to Big Al Fortin at the Banner. See if he'll hire me on as a stringer."

Todd must have seen it coming. Rubbing his bearded chin he joked, "Mind asking him if he has a job for me too?" He paused, then, in a more solemn voice, said, "I'll give you as many hours as I can, Mark, but full-time is out of the question right now. I hope things improve pretty soon, but if you find something full-time I won't blame you for taking it."

I wasn't serious about applying for work at the Banner when I said it. All I'd done was carpentry and I'm sure both of us assumed, although it remained unstated, that I'd be looking for work with one of Todd's competitors in the construction business.

That evening, in spite of lacking much in the way of either hope or enthusiasm for it, I compiled a list of local contractors. Of course, apart from the severe downturn in the economy, early-winter was the worst time of year to be looking for construction work. Another big problem: there weren't all that many contractors and I eliminated each one almost as quickly as I wrote the name down. Two were rumored to be critically short on work and purportedly planning to lay off soon; a couple of others had such poor reputations that I didn't want to be associated with them. Another contractor, although known for high quality work, couldn't keep help due of his miserable disposition. Todd was the best and I sure enjoyed working for him.

I tried picturing myself doing other types of work. Kitchen help in a restaurant? Driving delivery truck, maybe for one of the auto parts stores? Maybe. Almost everything I could think of, though, would be low paying and likely part-time. Also days. I guess I mostly clung to the hope that Todd's business would improve so that I could go back full-time. If that didn't happen but he could continue giving me at least some hours then a second part-time job might be the best answer. Particularly if the job were at night.

Thinking of night work, I remembered my off-hand remark to Todd about applying at the Collinsville Banner. Al's paper routinely included coverage of meetings— generally held at night—of town select boards, planning commissions, zoning boards, and school boards within about a twenty-mile radius of Collinsville. While meeting minutes and "officials' reports" appeared to be the source of many articles, other stories carried by-lines, indicating Al had paid to have the events covered in person by stringers. That was something I could picture myself doing; the more I thought about it the better I liked the idea.

"Big" Al Fortin earns the size modifier to his name. He's coarse-featured, tall—probably six-four—large-framed, heavy with muscle half-turned to flab and totally bald. Al looks like a man better-suited to a wrestling ring than sitting behind a desk at a newspaper office. I didn't know him well at all the day I stopped by, only from seeing him around town I guess, and dropping Todd's ad off a couple of times.

I felt my face flush when I told him I didn't have any professional writing experience.

"Well, Mark, we all started somewhere." A deep, smoker's voice with traces of the gruffness Al was noted for having.

I told him my mother had been a high school English teacher—"for what it's worth"—that she'd always taken pains to teach me proper grammar as I'd grown up. Also, that I'd done well in an English course I took that year in college. "Pulled an 'A' in fact."

"Think you can forget all you learned?"

I must have frowned.

"'Cause this ain't creative writing. What, where, when, how. Just the facts. Simple. Straightforward. Fifth grade words. Could be ninth grade at this point considering the illiterate ignoramuses the schools are turning out these days."

I didn't leave with a job but Al told me I could attend a school board meeting the following evening and write up a news story which he would consider buying for that week's issue. A rocky beginning, or so I thought. After we had become good friends, Al confessed to giving me a hard time that afternoon. "I had to see what you were made of, whether you were tough enough to follow through."

Follow through I did. As luck would have it the Collinsville school directors at their meeting unwittingly boosted my chances of selling that first story.

Only a handful of people attended: the three school board members, the school principal, the district superintendent, two teachers and myself. Except for the superintendent, I knew them all. No one bothered asking me why I was there but in view of what happened I suppose they assumed I had come only in a parental role, as both Molly and Seth attended Collinsville Elementary. I sat off to the side, feigning boredom, ostensibly doodling but actually taking copious notes, including quotations.

The two teachers, in a matter listed on the agenda, were seeking the board's blessing of a proposed field trip for seventh and eighth graders to a science museum. Predictably, it passed without much adieu by unanimous vote. The teachers thanked the board and left.

About then I expected someone would ask me my purpose in being there but still no one did. Instead, the principal and superintendent slid their chairs closer around the table so their backs were toward me, forming a sort of intimate huddle with the three school directors, and in hushed tones they resumed discussion. I caught some of it, bits and pieces about a "budget hole as large as… hundred thousand," the phrases "can't we pad enough…" and "keep it from getting out."

I stood up, walked closer to the front and took a chair nearest the table. That elicited notice. Also, finally, the question regarding why I was there.

Al printed my story as the lead in the next issue of the Collinsville Banner. I thought he might, which was why I badgered the folks around the table until they threw me out by declaring an executive session. Why I waited until it was over to get comments afterward (no one made any) and why I spent three hours at the town clerk's office the next morning sifting through dry school enrollment and budget data. I'd known a fair amount about Al's views from reading his paper, that he was a champion for transparency, freedom of information, full disclosure regarding governmental affairs at every level. I knew that Al was obsessed with holding public officials accountable for their actions.

Al isn't demonstrative when it comes to handing out praise but his prominent placement of my story suggested I'd scored. I'm sure it pleased him that the story was picked up by both large regional papers and at least one radio station, in each instance with proper source attribution to the Banner. The story opened up a can of worms which, within weeks, led to the resignations of two of the school directors. It all boiled down to collective incompetence and an effort to conceal the truth rather than embezzlement or any out and out corruption. As always, the taxpayers suffered the most, saddled with a nearly two hundred thousand dollar budget deficit.

I'd hit the jackpot with that first story but it set the bar high. Only through hard effort ever since had I managed to sustain that level of accurate, relevant, in-depth reporting. My by-line had appeared on the front page of the Banner in nearly every issue, often twice during an active news week. Al didn't pay much. I knew he couldn't. But added to my reduced wages from Todd I'd kept my head above water. Yes, I'd even faithfully met my child support obligation without having to resort to getting a modification for reduction from the court, the worst kind of hassle imaginable.

# 2

THE WEATHER IN Vermont that spring and early summer had been unbelievably bad for anyone needing to work outside. Colder than normal temperatures had lingered well into May; it had rained two out of every three days from the end of April through mid-June. As Todd pointed out, if there hadn't been a recession to cripple his business, the same amount of damage would have occurred due to the poor weather. We worked several dry Saturdays and Sundays to get caught up after mid-week rain.

Unfortunately, that erratic work schedule messed up the "chiseled-in-stone" child visitation schedule, resulting in my missing time with my kids, Molly and Seth. I was legally entitled to have them every other weekend—more often only at Ellen's discretion—but of course couldn't the weekends I worked. True to form, Ellen refused to be flexible regarding changes to the schedule. I missed Seth's staring role in a fifth grade play and Molly's dance recital in June due to Ellen's stubbornness. A classic Catch Twenty-two: I needed to work to pay the child support yet because I worked I couldn't spend as much time with the kids.

I'd have to say that missing time with Seth that spring into summer bothered me the most. At age eleven, Seth was a delight. Still wide-eyed, inquisitive and full of energy, he brightened my life as nothing else could. We took my canoe out to Tyler Pond a couple of times in May, which was good but a far cry from the previous summer when we'd gone fishing or simply boating at least every other week—even more often in between, when we'd invited Ellen's dad, Harry. I took Seth shopping once and we mountain-hiked but weeks went by when we didn't get to spend two days in a row together.

That was a low period for me but to be honest I have to include Harry in the mix of things gone wrong. We, the kids and I, didn't have Harry to share our lives with, at least not in the same way that we had the summer before.

I'll always remember the previous summer as one of the best of my life. The kids and I loved "Grandpa Harry." My ex-father-in-law, having suffered two heart attacks and a stroke, knew his life would likely be cut short. Blanche, his wife of thirty-three years, had lost her struggle with breast cancer two years earlier and Harry had soon after sold his plumbing and heating business, easily the largest in the three-county region. He was probably as relaxed that summer, as free from care, as he had ever been, certainly within my knowing him and probably at any time during his marriage to Blanche. A kind, caring, gentle man, he'd laughed and joked and told us, generally Seth and me, one story after another, many of them set in the days of his youth and early adulthood.

Although Harry was shrewd and had obviously done very well in business, his core values—rooted in fairness, frugality, and modesty—had remained untainted by financial success. Blanche could put on airs, spend a hundred thousand of Harry's money on an addition to the house (including a renovated kitchen with marble countertops), dress in the latest designer fashions, but you knew Harry would still have been just as happy sporting rags and living in a bungalow.

One of the qualities I especially admired in Harry was his blindness toward social and occupational caste. His egalitarian philosophy. Always a worker himself, he appreciated the efforts of a competent, friendly waitress or waiter, and always left generous tips. Depending upon how many times Blanche had complained, sent her steak back to the kitchen or how badly she had demeaned or embarrassed restaurant staff, Harry's tip could range as high as thirty-five percent, which of course outraged Blanche when he occasionally failed at keeping his generosity a secret. In Harry's book, there was nobility in every type of work in the world; the greatest of leaders, physicists or doctors were no better than the lowliest of laborers—they and their work all needed to be treated with the same degree of respect and dignity.

In some amazing way, each of those treasured occasions with Harry and the kids that previous summer had highlighted a different, unique facet of who he was. Each time we got together Harry would surprise us with a special memory, a capsulized bit of wisdom, or a poignant story from his past—one we'd never heard before—always in relatable terms to the kids.

Time was of the essence. Harry must have intuitively sensed it. He didn't lecture or preach but in his usual gentle, inimitable, bantering style he managed to express a wealth of life lessons. As school started at summer's end, as the leaves colored and fell and the days grew cooler, I looked back and cherished the time we'd spent with Harry.

In November, just before I started working for the Collinsville Banner, Harry had suffered a massive stroke. It had robbed him of speech and left him all but totally paralyzed. I knew nothing about the arrangements, of course, because Ellen and I were hardly speaking but Harry had ended up at the Collinsville Health and Rehabilitation Center. I felt sick over it and I know the kids did, especially Seth. Since then I'd visited the home as often as I could, taking Seth along if it was a day I had him. My feelings about it were mixed. Was it good for the kids to see a man so recently vibrant and loving now confined to a bed or propped in a chair? A man unable to speak intelligibly, barely able to smile; staring out with vacant eyes, perhaps not even comprehending what was said or going on in the room? I didn't know. Everyone has to learn the cruel facts of life yet my paternal instinct was to shield the kids from the cruelest of them for as long as possible. Harry did seem to brighten whenever I stopped in, especially if I had one or both kids along, so I figured that was probably the more important consideration. Such as it was, Harry's remaining life would certainly be of short duration.

Molly and I had never been close and that spring our relationship progressively worsened. For weeks I tried overlooking her increasingly disrespectful behavior toward me; over time I dreaded our being together. I wanted to believe she was simply going through a phase, one typical of American girls in adolescence. Laying it on the divorce was easy too, but in that case why didn't she hate her mother as well? As far as I could tell she remained on loving, respectful terms with Ellen. Why didn't she hate us both?

A fuller picture had emerged when I had both kids one Saturday evening in mid-June. Molly had placed her iPhone on the kitchen table as we sat eating.

"Expecting a call?" I asked in what I hoped was a light tone.

"Maybe," Molly said. "Or maybe I'll want to call Mom to come and get me."

"Oh?"

"She said I don't need to stay here if I don't want to."

"Is that right?" I hated the smarmy, know-it-all expression on her face. In that moment I saw a carbon copy of Ellen.

She nodded. "Yup. She said this place must be a real dump and I don't have to stay if I don't want to."

"I'm sorry to hear that," I said.

"She said you probably have bed bugs here."

"She did, did she? Well, you'll be happy to know there aren't any bedbugs. You may tell her."

"So she'll come and get me if I call. Or Alan will."

"Alan?"

She nodded. Insolent glare. Jaw defiant. I wanted in the worst way to smack the child.

I said, "You do whatever you need to do after we eat. Right now the phone comes off the table. Now, Molly!"

A brief, intense stare-down. She blinked.

Seth looked over at me, pale, eyes cast down.

After we had eaten, Molly shut herself in "her room," the only bedroom. (I always offered the decrepit pull-out sofa to Seth but always slept on it myself when he would claim to prefer his sleeping bag on the floor.

Seth watched a DVD film, an animated horror flick with a cast of creepy, reptile-green monsters. Later, just before we dozed off to sleep, he said in the darkness, "Dad, Molly didn't mean what she said. About..." he trailed off.

A lump in my throat. "I know. Hey?"

"What?"

"Thanks, buddy."

"You're welcome." A pause, then, "Oh, Dad?"

"Yes, son."

"I don't like Alan."

"Oh? Well, I don't know him. I've never even heard of Alan."

"I bet you won't like him."

"Thanks for the heads up, bud."

"You're welcome."

"Night, son."

"Night, Dad."

As they say, kids don't come with instruction manuals. Everyone has his or her own opinions about parenting. What to do and what not to do. You can get the latest advice reading books written by the experts or watch Dr. Phil on television but in the end I think it comes down to trial and error guided by common sense. Throw the gradual disintegration of a marriage, separation, and the finality of a divorce into the mix and you've lost the common sense part in what looks like a perfect recipe for child rearing disaster. Sometimes I wonder how any kid manages to emerge into adulthood half-way normal.

I know the cliche: Failed marriages are always fifty-fifty. With us it was a case of conflicting values. Ellen took after her mother while I guess I must be a bit like Harry was, easy going, not caring so much about money or the opinion of neighbors. I'd hoped she could resist using our kids as weapons but that was not to be.

# 3

LENNY'S BROWN PAPER bag served as a table ornament for nearly a week, reminding me of the failed-brakes incident each time I glanced at it yet not quite spurring me to action. I considered talking with Collinsville's police chief but hadn't gotten around to doing it. Something Al said that next Friday afternoon when I stopped by for my paycheck actually triggered my mentioning the matter to him. I had emailed him a news story the day before about a contentious select board meeting, in it quoting verbatim an inflammatory, possibly slanderous remark made by one of the selectmen.

"These people seem to think we don't have ears," Al said, peering over his reading glasses and up at me from his seat at the desk.

"Or that we won't dare print the idiot things they say."

He nodded. "Yeah. It's a wonder we haven't both been shot." He paused. "Oh, before I forget, Mark. Would you be willing to do the Street Talk column next week? Maggie wants to give it a break."

"Sure." Sounded good to me, an additional two or three hours of pay in the next check and probably easy to do, although I hadn't yet done the popular front page feature which consisted of brief comments of a half dozen or so citizens interviewed at random on Collinsville's Main Street. "Any particular topic or just leave it at whatever they want to say?"

"Hell, I don't know. Maggie usually leaves it open unless there's some burning issue of the day or week. Maybe see how it goes."

"What about the wind project? Looks like that could be heating up again."

"Ah…" he hesitated for several seconds before answering. "You could. I'm sick of hearing about it but I noticed they've started clear-cutting up on the ridge. State hasn't ruled yet on the project but I guess there's no crime in cutting. Assuming they have a logging permit."

"Yeah, I saw a couple of Dornier Logging skidders headed toward the mountain last week." I paused, my thoughts shifting to another matter which I'd finally decided to bring up. "Something you just said, Al."

"Yeah?"

"About being shot? Mind if…" I motioned toward the chair, the only other piece of furniture in the tiny, cluttered office which fronted Main Street. Al rented this and a larger connected room in the back in which the newspaper's layout was done.

"Sure, Mark." As I sat he removed his glasses, set them on the desk next to an overflowing ashtray and rubbed his eyes. I was relieved. Trying to talk to Al while he stares at you over the top rim of his reading glasses can be distracting. You wonder if he's rushed and hoping you'll finish quickly so he can get back to something he considers more important.

"It's probably nothing," I said. "No connection with any of my stories, I mean, but…" I told him about my brakes failing and what Lenny had said, including that he couldn't be one hundred percent certain they were tampered with. I said I'd given it quite a bit of thought off and on ever since but had come up dry. "Scary," I concluded, "not knowing whether to take it seriously."

Al had leaned back in the swivel chair, his frown deepening as he'd listened. There was a minute or two of silence in the room. Well, not total silence: Through the one small, screened and partially opened window came the usual mid-July street sounds, cars passing, air brakes from what sounded like a large semi, a couple of kids squabbling on the sidewalk then fading away.

"Yeah, Mark, I'd take it seriously," Al said, rocking forward, clasping his hands and leaning his elbows on the desk. "I'd take it very seriously."

I didn't like the ominous tone of his voice. "So...what are you thinking?" I heard the slight tremor in my own voice.

"First, the obvious, something both of us know. Namely that a few folks are always unhappy over the things we report. I know you've had your share of run-ins with people who didn't like being quoted. Or didn't want the facts to come out."

"Sure, but—"

"And so have I. Lots of them. They'll button-hole me in a store or on the street. Tell me the paper stinks. Cancel their subscriptions. Incidentally," he said with a trace of a smile, "that's always a tip-off we're doing a good job. When somebody cancels, or maybe tells me to go to hell, and then you see them buying the next issue at the mini-mart. I get a kick out of that."

"Makes it all seem worth doing, maybe?"

"Yeah, something like that. Anyway," he continued, his expression again serious, "we know we aren't universally liked in this town. People argue with us on the street and write hot-headed letters. Cancel subscriptions. Are they angry enough to mess with your brakes? Ninety-nine percent of them, no. Most of them just want to vent. Get it off their chests. Sometimes they'll be all friendly when you run into them a day or two later. Do I think a tiny percentage might go further? Unfortunately," he said, nodding resolutely, "I do."

His dark tone of voice made me gulp. "So you think..."

"That we're living in a scary time. A period of reduced civility. Reduced tolerance for diversity, especially out here in the sticks. A lot of rednecks. Also, scariest of all, I see a growing number of people who lack the normal inhibitions which keep most of us from taking direct action. I don't know if video games are to blame or what but a lot of people, especially young people, think it's okay to act out their anger. Resort to violence as a right. I hope I'm wrong, Mark, but I've got to say I don't like the sound of it. This business about your brakes."

I couldn't think how to respond. Had I expected him to question Lenny's judgment? Had I hoped he'd discount the possibility of a disgruntled reader turning homicidal? Al obviously took it seriously; in my mind he had validated the threat. I decided to put the rest of it on the table.

"Al," I said, breaking the long silence, "there's something else I should mention. It may not be important, but…"

"Shoot," he said, his eyes widening encouragingly.

"It has to do with salad dressing. I'm sure I've mentioned before how allergic I am to peanuts? Well, any nuts, really, but peanuts are the worst."

He nodded. "You told us that when we celebrated Maggie's birthday, remember? I brought in that big box of chocolates and you wouldn't eat one because of the warning on the label."

"That's right," I said, recalling our little office party. "Even if there aren't any nuts in them the equipment can have traces of nut oil and for somebody as sensitive as I am it can be deadly. So anyway, one night I was fixing myself a salad. I poured on one of my favorite dressings, which has olive oil and vinegar as a base and a lot of spices like basil and garlic. Oh, and tomato, too."

"Sounds good."

"It is. Except that when I sat down to eat the salad it didn't smell right. I smelled peanut oil. I went back to the bottle and poured some out to make sure it wasn't the lettuce or one of the other vegetables. Sure enough, it had a distinct peanut smell. That wasn't one of the ingredients, of course, because I'm anal when it comes to checking labels in the store. I thought I had to be crazy. I even waited a few minutes and sniffed again. As much as I wanted to eat the salad, I ended up throwing it and the bottle of dressing into the garbage."

"Was it a new bottle?"

"No, that's the funny thing. I'd already used some of it. Maybe a quarter or a third. Which meant it had to be okay a few days earlier. I'd had the kids over the weekend before and I remember fixing them salads. I'd had three or four other salad dressings on hand, including French, which they both like, and I'd opened this new bottle for my own salad. I know it probably sounds foolish, Al, but when you've lived for as long as I have with this nut allergy it goes beyond being an obsession. I mean, your life depends on your making the right decisions."

Nodding, Al said, "Oh, I know. I've read about it. Heard about it."

"You go into anaphylactic shock. Can't breath. Heart rate plummets. That's why I always carry a bee sting kit. Epinephrine. I have to shoot it in fast, too. I've had a couple of scary close calls. Even then I suffer for a week afterward."

"So who knows about your peanut allergy?"

I thought for a moment. "Just about everybody who knows me very well. Any time I'm eating out or socializing where there's food. Even snacks. I'd have to say it's common knowledge, just as you know."

"Hmmm. So assuming you didn't imagine it—"

"Which is a possibility, I'll freely admit. But I double checked. Actually waited a few minutes and then sniffed again to make sure. The thing is, Al, I've had to be so careful over the years that I think I've developed a heightened sense for detecting it. Sounds crazy, I know, but I trust my sense of smell, at least for peanut oil, more than my hearing or eyesight."

"Okay, so I guess the dressing had to have been tampered with in your apartment. Who'd have access?"

"Nobody. Well, except for the landlord. Keith Dornier."

"You always lock the door?"

"Always. I'm not in the best of company, you know. There's a bunch of kids, late teens, early twenties, next to me. That one's a revolving door. New kids in and out every few days. And on the other side a couple of welfare moms, and then upstairs...well, more of the same. Wouldn't dream of not locking my door."

"The door wasn't jimmied."

"No."

"Would you say it's easily pickable?"

"Oh, sure. One of those light metal el-cheapo jobs, key in the knob. Eminently pickable."

"Hmm. Anything look different? In your apartment, I mean."

"No. Nothing obvious anyway. But then, that was before I..."

"Right." He paused, looking down reflectively for a moment. "Okay, so, back to the brakes," he said, facing me, "Any idea where or when somebody could have messed with them? In your parking lot, for example?"

"Oh, sure. The parking's all at the other end of the building. Another thing. Nobody'd pay any attention to a guy stretched on his back under a pickup. Most of the rigs are like mine, old and falling apart. It looks like a pitstop for a demolition derby out there most of the time."

"Hmm," Al said. He made a motion as though intending to reach for a cigarette, but then drew back, perhaps because I was there. He's considerate that way. We all know he's a chain smoker but most of the time he resists lighting up when any of us are with him in the tiny front office.

Taking it as a signal, I pushed back a little in the chair. Starting to get up, I said, "Al, I don't mean to dump this on you. I guess I just thought I should tell somebody, and—"

"No, Mark," he said, gesturing for me to remain. "I'm trying to figure out what I'd do if I were in your place. I guess first, I'd go down and have a talk with Clem. Get him to write up a statement so it's at least on record."

"Makes sense. Even give him the cracked brake fittings." I'd already decided to stop by the Collinsville Police Chief's office but I didn't let on to Al.

"Right. Oh yeah, I'd give him the fittings. You know, it's really odd," he continued thoughtfully, "that it would be one of you guys. I've always known this could happen, some crackpot working himself into such a lather that he turns violent. But I figured I'd be the target, you know what I mean? Not one of you. You and Maggie. Well Grace too. You do one hell of a good job tracking down the news. You especially, Mark. I'm not much for handing out awards, but...well...I really appreciate your work." A bit more hoarseness had crept into his voice.

"Thanks, Al."

"No, seriously. It's the hard-hitting, investigative stuff that's behind the increases in ads and circulation. People want to know what's really going on. Not just what the town officers feel like saying. You go out and ask the right questions, the same ones everybody wants asked. And you generally get the answers. People appreciate that."

"Most of the time."

"Well, sure. We're always going to step on a few toes. Bound to. I'm just sorry it's come to this. I feel awful that you're the target not me. I'm the one who sounds off in editorials. By good rights I should be the one to take any backlash." Al's disappointed tone suggested his regrets stemmed less from the fact that someone out there seemed bent on murder than that he wasn't the intended victim, the object of a possible life and death struggle.

I heard the unmistakable sincerity in his voice but I wondered at his logic. How many people faithfully read his weekly editorials and of those how many believed his opinions mattered? I guess when you put yourself out there week after week, expressing personal opinions on a wide range of controversial issues—as opposed to simply reporting facts in news stories—you might develop an inflated sense of your writing's importance.

"You certainly raise hackles, Al," I said diplomatically.

"Well, let's just say there's rarely any doubt as to where I stand."

"None whatsoever. Now I need to figure out whose hackles I've raised."

"Yeah, of course," he said, frowning, "that's what we need to focus on. What issue, what motive. Who gains."

"Exactly. I've thought about it ever since the bakes failed and I can name half a dozen people pissed off with me over things I've written. Trouble is, I can't picture any of them doing anything like this."

Al nodded reflectively. "Jeff Smith, for example. He wasn't happy with either one of us when those pieces came out."

"That's an understatement," I said, chuckling over memory of the nursing home administrator's reaction to my three-part series detailing a pattern of geriatric neglect, mistreatment and exploitation at his facility. Although the facts I'd used were indisputable, in a letter to the editor which Al published, Smith countered that I had grossly distorted them, blurring the chronology of widely occurring incidents by lumping them together and presenting various facts and statements out of context. He denied several subjective claims made by two of my cited sources and had promised immediate remedial action to correct a few acknowledged but—he'd claimed—insignificant deficiencies. (Smith wasn't the only one angry at me. My darling ex had blasted me over the phone, saying, "Thanks, you son of a bitch! Now they'll probably torture my father!")

Al was counting Jeffrey out. "He speaks to me now," he said, "plus he's started advertising for help again."

"And will always need to," I quipped, "unless and until he starts treating his help with more respect." (Three of my sources had been disgruntled former employees of the Collinsville Health and Rehabilitation Center.)

Neither one of us, however, could imagine Jeffrey Smith crawling under my truck and monkeying with the brakes or picking a lock to adulterate my salad dressing with peanut oil.

We both agreed Henri Renaud was an equally improbable suspect. No one could have gotten angrier than Henri had been over my

Renaud Construction story printed in mid-April, a piece that helped trigger an investigation, still in progress, into the company's alleged shoddy workmanship on the new wing of the Collinsville Elementary School. However, as Al said, "Henri was feisty and loud for awhile but once he got it out of his system I doubt he still harbors that strong a grudge."

"Plus he's fighting on too many fronts," I pointed out. "Todd tells me the condo association at Tamarack Peak is suing Henri for all that crappy work he did up there. I'm sure they'll make it stick." I had intimate knowledge of how bad the work was: Todd was the successful bidder on a portion of the rehab work following the flooding of four Blue Spruce units. Water pipes along the north-facing walls of two of the units had frozen and burst, sending thousands of gallons of water cascading down three floors and through common walls into adjoining units. For insurance purposes we'd photographed all four units before and during the gutting of them, in stages as we'd removed the water-soaked wallboard, ceilings and carpeting. The photographs documented better than words the builder's lousy work, most significantly including insulation gaps large enough to throw a cat through.

"Incidentally, what was the final tally up there?" Al asked.

"I never heard a total," I said, "but I know they were estimating as high as seventy-five thousand per unit. Everything had to be replaced, even the appliances."

Al whistled. "A lot of money."

"Sure is." I paused, uncertain whether I should come out with the name I was thinking. Attempting to sound more facetious than serious, I continued, "We were speaking a minute ago about the wind project. Sounds far-fetched, maybe, but what about the Dornier clan? I don't mean Donald himself, but one of his boys."

Al's frown formed a question.

I went on: "You know how Roger felt about the article I did on that gun control bill. You didn't take a stand but I think I told you he button-holed me, told me I'd blown it out of proportion. Called me every name in the book."

"Well, I knew he wasn't happy, Mark, but…"

"And I probably forgot to mention it, but I heard Little Don went ballistic over my last article about the wind project. First, the fact that he's the majority investor in the LLC which owns the land up there. But supposedly what put him over the edge was our printing the fact that he has a large stake in the wind project itself. In the company."

"Oh?"

I nodded. "Think back, Al. Until the article, until you printed it, his name hadn't been mentioned anywhere in connection with the wind project. Sure, we all assumed he'd be the one hired to clear-cut the summit area for the turbine towers. Certainly the access road up the mountain. And I think most of us assumed either Little Don or his dad owned the land. Even though it's listed in another corporate name on the deed at the Town Clerk's Office. What most us never suspected, at least I didn't until I went digging, was that he's part owner of the development company itself."

"He couldn't hold that against us, Mark," he said, with a trace of defensiveness. "I mean, it's public information."

"Public information not widely known, though, because that was the way he wanted it. I only found out the connection by contacting the Secretary of State's Office and asking who they had listed as principals in both LLCs."

Al considered it for moment. "Okay, but now that it's commonly known, what motive could he have for…"

"Silencing me?"

"Right. Except vengeance. Which would be stupid. You and I don't always agree with the Dornier boys but you have to admit they aren't stupid. None of them would take that kind of chance."

"I agree they aren't stupid. And getting even isn't a strong enough motive. But let's just suppose there are some other facts he'd rather not have made public. Now that he knows I'm willing to dig a little deeper wouldn't you expect him to get nervous? Scared I'll dig them up?"

"Well, I suppose. If there are any other facts. A big if, but anything's possible." Al's tone suggested the possibility deserved a ranking of Remote. He glanced down at his desk for a second, then looked back up at me. "If you'd rather stop covering it, Mark," he said, his voice lower and more hoarse, "I'll certainly understand. Hell, I don't want to see you getting killed over it."

"No, I'm not suggesting I want to back away from it. I was just throwing the name out there along with the others. Old man Dornier wouldn't do anything like it, of course. But the boys...well, they can be rough around the edges as you know. Roger and Little Don especially."

"Can be, for sure. But even Little Don wouldn't stoop to anything like this. No way. In fact I saw him in one of the stores only a couple of days ago. Seemed fine to me. And Roger hasn't pulled his ad. Hell, not only that, when I stopped in on Wednesday he bought a half-page spread for next week. Got a sale on for ammo at the shop."

A distinct tautness had entered Al's tone of voice: I had evidently struck a nerve. If I could have rerun the previous ten minutes I would have avoided any mention of the Dornier boys.

I said, "And I guess I can't imagine them crawling under a pick-up truck to bugger the brakes either, any more than I can the others. Or breaking into an apartment to adulterate salad dressing." No point in reminding him that I'd just said my landlord, Keith, the next to the youngest of the four Dornier brothers and owner of the apartment building, had a key.

Tension in the tiny room eased slightly. It wasn't the first time I'd encroached on sacred territory with Al. His bravado has its limits, ending shy of risking the loss of a major advertiser. Take too firm a stand on certain issues and he'd risk economic suicide. The Dornier family goes back at least three generations in Collinsville, are among its most respected citizens and have tentacles reaching deeply into the economy of the community.

"So," I said, leaning forward in the chair, "I guess about all I can do is wait. Be on guard, see if anything else happens. Anyway, thanks for hearing my tale of woe." I stood up and turned toward the door.

"Oops," he said, "don't forget." He reached for an envelope on top of a disorderly pile of papers beside his computer keyboard. and handed it up to me. "Wish I could pay you what you're worth, Mark."

"Thanks, Al. I'm glad you don't. I'd need a third job to make ends meet."

He gave me a faint smile then, a relief as I hated to leave on so sour a note. "Hey, let me give it some thought," he said. "Poke around. Never can tell what you hear if you keep your ears open. Oh, and I'd be sure to talk with Clem."

"I will. Thanks Al." I didn't look back to see him light up.

It turned out that my visit with Collinsville Police Chief Clem McDonald would need to wait as his cruiser was absent from the parking space next to his office on Elm Street. Oddly, I felt more relieved than disappointed. I still had nothing substantial to go on and after my conversation with Al it seemed that I might be making a mountain out of a mole hill. Sure, Al had taken it all seriously but he hadn't added anything to what I'd already gone over in my own mind. Little did I know how quickly circumstances could change.

# 4

ECONOMIC STIMULUS DOLLARS, tens of billions of them, had supposedly gushed from the bankrupt federal treasury two years earlier, pouring into all fifty states, but in the tiny state of Vermont any evidence of their longer-term effect was hard to be found. The state's unemployment rate, although three or four percentage points below the national average, had remained high. Locally, due not only to the poor economy over-all but to a virtually snow-less ski season, the Tamarack Peak Corporation trimmed its summer work force further than usual, curtailing what some in town, especially laid-off workers, claimed were critically necessary maintenance functions. (One remark often heard: "You couldn't pay me enough to ride one of those lifts next winter!")

It was at the end of the workday on a Friday at the end of June, a day or two after my talk with Al, when Todd Drake told me he'd have to let me go entirely due to the still worsening slump in construction. I think he fought off breaking down as he told me. His son, Ben, just out of high school and normally the most friendly, outgoing kid you could work alongside, had obviously taken it hard as well, escaping to the cab of his dad's pickup truck to avoid our usual end-of-the-week, always libationary ritual of bull-banter at the tailgate.

"When things get better..." Todd said, sounding hopeful, but I sensed by his firm handshake as we parted that he didn't expect to be calling me back. At least not any time soon. Lately, apparently in jest, he'd mentioned the possibility of their having to go to work for someone else. I think he was actually trying it on for size, probably knowing it wouldn't fit for him, knowing he might lose his son as a workmate, yet seeing it as their only option given the bleak economic reality.

For several months I'd faced the prospect of being laid off entirely, of having to re-file my unemployment claim and go about finding another job. What I hadn't foreseen, however, was the emotional toll it would take when it finally happened. I'd worked seventeen years for Todd, ever since my year at college. We were a well-matched team, made even better when Ben had joined us a few weeks earlier, adding brute strength, youthful energy and his own great sense of humor. I guess I'd never given much thought to the importance of my carpentry job beyond its being a source of income. Never realized the extent to which the workplace camaraderie had contributed to my emotional well-being. The lay-off left me with a hollow feeling, an emptiness much like that I'd felt after moving out of our home, leaving the kids with Ellen.

Three or four days later I did follow through with paying a visit to Clem McDonald. Unfortunately, over the course of the week since I'd talked with Al, the potential gravity of the failed brakes and the tainted salad dressing had wained, giving way now to a mounting anxiety over the more immediate challenge of finding a job. I know my presentation lacked a convincing urgency. Clem listened, appeared attentive and nodded encouragingly as I related what had happened, yet I read skepticism in his face. Perhaps it was that almost imperceptible knitting of his heavy brows.

"I see what Lenny meant," he said, holding the brake fitting toward the light from his florescent desk lamp, "but it's all corroded around here, pitted pretty deep too. Could have just been ready to break." He turned it over, examining it from every angle.

Clem McDonald is a soft-spoken man, short, stocky in build, mid-sixties, with heavy jowls and an even disposition. He's been police chief so long he had to have dealt with the parents of the current crop of juvenile delinquents back when they were the same age. Maybe even the grandparents. As easy-going as he seems, Clem has a reputation for toughness when circumstances demand it, but I've never seen that side of him.

"Now about this salad dressing," he said, setting the brake fitting down. "You said you threw the bottle away?"

"Yeah. I didn't want it around. That was before the problem with the brakes. Before I suspected anything. Peanut oil wasn't listed as an ingredient so I just figured it had to be something wrong with my nose. When you're as sensitive as I am you never take chances. I didn't read all that much into it at the time because, as I say, this was a couple of weeks before the brake incident." My voice sounded dull to me, devoid of intensity. Doubts seemed to have crept in since I'd discussed the matter with Al. I remembered feeling more charged that day, feeling that both the salad dressing and the brake failure were significant whereas today in my recounting of the incidents to the police chief they struck me as frivolous. Yes, I could have been mistaken about the peanut smell just as Lenny could have been about the brakes.

Clem gave me an objective, fair hearing; I can't fault him. He agreed to write up a statement for his files and of course asked me to be sure to report any further suspicious incidents.

It was on Saturday of that same week—a weekend which Molly had refused to spend with me—when I learned the news from Seth that Ellen's friend, Alan, had moved into the house with them, moved in with his clothes, a rifle, and boxes of "stuff." Seth wasn't at all happy about it.

What a surprise. I tried my best not to register any reaction.

"Hey buddy, you remember we talked about all that. About when people get divorced. That even though they have kids together they have a right to...well, find somebody else to be with. It could happen with me, you know, and looks like it's happened with your mom. Which is good if it makes her happy."

"I still don't like him."

"Well, unfortunately, your mom is free to choose her friends. Unless he does something to you. I mean something bad." I paused. "Ah, he hasn't, has he?"

Glancing down, he shook his head. "No," he said, then more earnestly, looking up, "but Dad, did you know he smokes?"

"Well, I've never met him so I can't say I know anything about him. So he smokes, does he?"

He nodded, scowling.

I said, "Yuk. I hope he doesn't smoke in the house." Ellen had evidently lowered her standards there. Neither one of us had ever smoked and we'd impressed it upon the kids that smoking was a foul, unhealthy and costly habit best avoided.

"Only a little, but Mom says she won't let him smoke in her car. She doesn't like it in the house either but she let's him some. He's only supposed to do it in your...in the den with the door closed."

"Good. You kids shouldn't have to breathe cigarette smoke. The den, huh?" I imagined the small den, my favorite room in the house. My refuge. Dark, masculine, paneled floor to ceiling in polished butternut. I'd worked long and painstakingly hard in getting the walls to that deep, lustrous finish only found on the highest quality wood furniture. I imagined it now reeking of tobacco smoke. The bastard!

"Yeah, just the den. And she's trying to make him quit."

"Good. I hope she can get him to. It's a dirty habit."

I didn't ask any more questions regarding their new household member. It wasn't right putting Seth on the spot. I was distracted, though, for the rest of the evening, thinking about a man named Alan now living in the same household with my son. Someone my son didn't like and who was making him unhappy. A man who would be influencing him, if only slightly, as a male role model. I could hardly condemn the guy strictly on the basis of his smoking (even doing it in my den) but I wondered what else I might find objectionable about him.

Early in July the weather in Vermont changed dramatically. As though in response to the flipping of a switch, the cold, drizzly days—a full two month string of them—suddenly ended. Skies cleared, the wind pattern shifted from due north to west-southwest, bringing mercifully warm breezes.

This lifting of what had been an oppressive meteorological pall raised my spirits as well. Yes, I'd lost my carpentry job. But I still worked part-time for the Collinsville Banner, bringing in a few bucks each week. Add the unemployment benefits to that and I'd eat, maintain a roof over my head and keep from going to jail for non-payment of child support.

Sure, I had pared my spending to the barest minimum, even dropping internet service and taking my laptop to either the coffee shop or library to use the free wifi. But I'd gotten used to the inconvenience. That particular austerity measure, for example, had forced me out of the apartment to email my stories to Al or do research, often early in the morning following an evening meeting or late at night. That would Invariably lead to some social interaction— generally good for my spirits—which also often led to news leads.

One day, lured by the fine weather, I pumped up the tires on my bicycle, oiled and greased it, and scrubbed off the crud to reclaim a shine. It was a mid-priced, skinny-tired street model which I'd bought around the time we'd given Seth his first bike—with required training wheels— on his fifth birthday. My bike was an antique in the modern world of bikes and also something of an anomaly around Collinsville, a village with a growing reputation for its extensive, excellently laid out and maintained system of mountain biking trails. During the summer and late into the fall, mountain bikes are about all you see. (I have a theory: Fast-forward thirty years and a good many of these trail-sucking, twenty-something animals will be on kidney dialysis!)

It's funny how your perceptions change when you take to a bicycle. I found myself noticing things I hadn't seen, hadn't been aware of while driving: a house freshly painted, a sign marking the entrance to a new business, the earthy smell of newly-cut grass, the scent of blooming Day Lilies waving from a street-side flowerbed, the tranquility of lush meadows and rolling hills in myriad shades of summer green. I'd forgotten the benefits of riding. That you see and feel the world at a slower pace, that you exercise little-used muscles and wind yourself on hills, the equivalent of a workout at an expensive fitness club.

I had forgotten the social aspects as well. You can't pedal past someone you know sitting on his porch without at least waving, and usually you'll stop for a minute or two and comment on the weather or how good his garden looks. This often leads to deeper conversation, sometimes an invitation to join him on the porch, even a cold brewski if you're lucky. Certainly in years past—on those few occasions I'd managed to get out and do it—my bicycling hadn't provided the degree of social interaction I now realized was possible. Thinking back I remembered it was mostly solace I'd needed from biking, escape from squalling kids and a wife never satisfied with the amount of money I brought home or happy with either the quality or the rate of progress I made in restoring our house.

Ralph Swartz wasn't sitting on his porch the afternoon we renewed our friendship. He pulled up alongside me on South Main Street, riding his own bike, de rigueur a mountain bike.

"Hey man, what you been up to?" he called out.

I didn't recognize him at first in the blue riding helmet. The bushy mustache gave him away.

I told him not much. "Trying to stave off the flab."

I regretted the comment even as I said it. A glance at Ralph's lycra tank top and shorts told me he either hadn't tried staving off the flab or had tried and failed. About the same age as me, thirty-seven or eight, he'd changed little in facial appearance all the years I'd known him, all the years since I'd first met him when he'd worked a brief period as a laborer for Todd. He'd done okay and left with no hard feelings to take a route delivery job.

We'd been fairly good friends back then and for a while after he'd married a local girl named Julie. Our friendship hadn't thrived much past my marriage to Ellen, however, another local girl who'd gone to school with Julie and considered her socially inferior. (Apparently a girl whose father owns a plumbing and heating business is at the top of the social heap, at least the way it's stacked in tiny Collinsville.)

As we rode along, slower and side by side, Ralph said Julie and their three daughters were doing fine but that he'd recently been laid off from his bread delivery job. "Cutbacks in the routes," he said, glancing over. "Fifteen years and they tell me I have a choice of either moving to Portland, Maine, or taking a layoff. Selling the house would be near impossible the way the market is, even if we wanted to move, which we don't."

"Welcome to the club." Keeping it brief, I filled him in on my situation, ending with a comment about being thankful to at least have a part-time job with the Banner. He'd known of my writing for the paper. Said they'd always bought and read it.

"Julie appreciated your articles a few months back," he said as we slowed at the intersection with Elm Street. "The ones about the nursing home. She started working there just before they came out. And of course her great-grandfather's been in there for three," he paused for a moment, "no must be closer to four years now. Anyway, she kept saying you were dead on. Guess it made a difference, too. I mean it shook things up. She got something like a dime an hour raise right after that. They're giving her more notice, too. About her schedule, I mean."

"Good, glad to hear it. And thanks for telling me." He'd jogged my memory: It had been Julie I'd caught sight of a couple of times when I'd visited Harry at the home. I added, "We don't always get much feedback on our stories. Unless we misquote somebody. Or don't get the facts right." We pulled over to the sidewalk to let a car and then a light truck pass by. I turned and asked if I'd heard him right. "You said her great-grandfather?"

"Yeah. Old Asa Warren."

"Huh. Must be pretty old."

He nodded. "In fact he has a birthday coming up. I think she said a hundred and two. Supposed to be a little celebration next week...I think on Saturday after lunch."

"A hundred and two! Good lord!"

He nodded again. "Oh yeah. Miserable old cuss. He's already out-lived four of his five kids, including Julie's grandfather. Huge fam-ily but Julie says she'll probably be the only one in the whole family who'll be there on Saturday."

"That's sad," I said. I turned a second later and, chuckling, added, "So when he finally dies they'll probably need to hire a few paid mourners!"

Ralph smiled but I couldn't be sure he'd understood.

With the traffic cleared behind us for the moment, we resumed riding in tandem up South Main.

Suddenly an inspired thought. "Maybe I could cover it," I said. "Do a little feature story for the paper. Jeez, he has to be the oldest per-son in town. Hell, probably in the whole Northeast Kingdom."

"I expect he is. That would be nice, Mark," Ralph said looking across, "but do they still let you in the place? I mean after those articles?"

I laughed. "Haven't barred the door yet. I try to go in every other week or so to see Harry, Ellen's dad."

"That's good. I mean with you and...divorced now and all," he trailed off for a moment, then continued, "You and Harry's sister must be about the only family he sees."

"Is that right?"

"Off the record, that is. Confidentiality and all, as Julie's always saying. Lots of people go in and see him. Several who worked for him, according to Julie. But as far as family..." He didn't finish the sentence but his meaning was unmistakable.

I suspected that was the case. As Harry's only child, Ellen stood to inherit when he died but there'd be no financial incentive for her to squeeze in a visit while he lived. One of the nurse aides had also mentioned Harry's sister, Dorothy, but our visits apparently hadn't yet coincided. I remembered Harry speaking affectionately of "Dottie" many times over the years, that she was a widow, living in Burlington, Vermont. We'd actually met only once, at Blanche's funeral; given the confusion of that day, I wasn't certain I'd recognize her again.

As we pedaled along, I brought up the subject of raising daughters. "Must be rough," I said, "with three girls. One's hard enough."

Ralph took his time to answer; I wondered if it might be a sore subject. Finally, he said, "No, but you don't always know where you stand with them. They're very different. Kyla, the middle one, is the sweetest kid you could ask for. Little Carrie's spoiled rotten but still manageable. Sarah, on the other hand..." I looked over briefly and caught him shaking his head, "...typical teenager, I guess. Actually, I'd always hoped we'd have a son but Julie hasn't cooperated on that one."

"Hmm. Seems like I've heard it's the sperm that determines a kid's sex."

"Whatever. You're probably right."

I knew then by the dull tone in his voice that it was a sore subject.

We'd biked on in silence for another quarter of a mile or so when I reopened the topic of kids and parenting, telling him he was lucky. "At least you and Julie can join together in a united front. Ellen and I can't agree on a damn thing. The poor kids get stuck in the middle. Especially Seth. I went for custody of him but no dice. Not even split custody. Mother's rights and all that. I think even Harry wanted to weigh in on my side when it came to Seth but he couldn't quite go up against his own daughter."

"Huh. That's rough on your boy."

"Yeah, especially now that Ellen's found a...whatever he is. Alan somebody, according to Seth."

"Alan Ames."

"You know him?"

"No. Word gets around, that's all."

"Do you know anything about him? Like where he works?" I glanced over and caught the slight shrug of his shoulders.

"Not really. I think he's the one selling used cars out on route two. Young fellow, late twenties, maybe early thirties. Somebody said he banged himself up in a car accident a few years ago. Supposedly got a chunk of money in a settlement but blew through most of it. Kept enough to buy up a half-dozen used cars to sell. He may be the one I've seen tooling around in a bright red Corvette. Not a new one, but fancy looking."

"Doesn't sound like Ellen's type. Go figure, as they say."

"Can't be a lot of money in selling used cars, if that's what you mean."

"It is."

"That's all I know about him, anyway. Moved in with his sister at her place out there on Route Two just after the gas station and started selling used cars. I don't know much about her either except I think she's the one who works for those lawyers next to the hardware store. Hardy and Danforth."

"Huh. Well, according to my kids, Mr. Ames has now moved in with them. That's why I'm kind of curious. The only thing against him so far is that he smokes. I can't very well fault him on his lousy judgment in picking women."

Ralph gave a little chuckle and said, "No, I guess not."

"Well, he has my sympathy, poor sucker. Kind of makes me want to send him an anonymous warning. If he has any money left from his settlement he sure won't have it for long." I slowed the bike to put my foot down. We'd reached a "T" in the road, the intersection at the bottom of the hill below my apartment building, the scene of my near accident a few weeks earlier. "This is the end of the line for me," I said. "Got a cold one with your name on it up there in the fridge"

"Thanks, Mark," he said, glancing at his watch, "but it's time I headed back too."

"Hey, Ralph, I'm glad we got together. Maybe if...well, I'm going to have to do something to stay in shape, and—"

"Yeah, me too. They say when you're laid off you need to stick to a schedule. Get up just as early every day and so forth. I'm planning on hitting the road for an hour or so every good day we have."

"I'm thinking the same thing," I said. "Maybe tomorrow afternoon, say three-thirty?"

"Sure. Meet you right here?"

"Sounds good."

Back at the apartment I flipped open a can of Miller with my name on it. (Although I'd never been one to drink a whole lot of beer, on a weak impulse coinciding with the recent change toward milder weather I had splurged on a six pack.) As I sat on the sagging couch I felt a hundred percent better than when I'd left. The sunshine. The exercise. Meeting up with Ralph and hitting it off again as though there hadn't been a fifteen-year hiatus in our friendship. I felt great; only my calf muscles complained.

I made a mental note to check with Al regarding old Mr. Warren at the nursing home. Maggie wrote most of the human interest features and while I didn't want to step on her toes, I'd been thinking of branching out, mainly to improve the paycheck but also to expand my writing skills. If Al agreed and didn't view it as an encroachment on her territory it should be a story that would almost write itself, plus I'd get a chance to look in on Harry.

That weekend it was my turn to have the kids. I picked them both up on Saturday morning but had trouble from the start with Molly, who vetoed every activity I could think of. It was a beautiful, sunny day but she didn't want to do anything outside, not biking or hiking or going to a lake where there was a beach, or anything involving the out-of-doors. Back at my apartment as we discussed the matter of what to do, I grew increasingly frustrated having to compete with her iPhone for her attention. Any meaningful communication between Molly and me seemed out of the question.

I treated them to lunch at the nice little Chinese restaurant in town, in spite of Molly's declaration that her mother would never go there again because the food was so horrible—she quoted Ellen as having said they probably served "road-killed porcupines"—and then, after more unpleasant wrangling with her over her iPhone I suggested that perhaps she'd be happier spending the weekend with her mother.

She said she definitely would, adding, "...and with Alan. Mom and Alan. I think they're going to Walmart this afternoon."

I said, "Well, that's just ducky, Molly. Why don't you give your mother and Alan a call on that thing right now. Find out if I can drop you off back at home."

My relief was palpable a few minutes later when she got out of the truck and slammed the door shut in the driveway of her mother's showplace home on Hudson Road.

To be objective about it, I probably wasn't offering much in the way of appealing options. I had no idea what a girl—no, make that a teenage girl of...fourteen, was she?—would desire to do for entertainment on a weekend in July in company with her father and little brother. Not a clue. Worse yet, this wasn't just any young woman of fourteen, but my own daughter, someone I'd had a hand in raising, in nurturing.

Molly's slamming of the door, though a blessed relief at that moment, had an inescapable quality of finality to it. In a way, I thought, that sound and that gesture symbolized like nothing else could, our complete disconnectedness. I now knew so little about Molly Sloan that we were essentially strangers.

Ralph's comments about his daughters came to mind also, how he had simply shaken his head and said, "typical teenager, I guess," in describing his oldest. He had expressed disappointment at not having a son and as I looked over at my own son, settling himself more comfortably now on the roomier seat of the truck, I felt grateful.

As the weekend with Seth went along, I kept sensing that something was troubling him. He seemed unusually quiet at times, preoccupied. I thought at first it must be continued upset over his sister's little scene after lunch on Saturday but when we discussed Molly, when I told him she was going through a difficult stage in life, going from being a kid to a young woman and needed our understanding more than blame, he seemed fine with it. He'd noticed her infatuation with boys and it came out that Molly often back-talked her mother now, arguing mostly over staying out late and dating.

It wasn't until Sunday afternoon when Seth alluded to Alan's "promises" that the source of his real concern came out. I had asked him about Alan's rifle, whether it was like my .30-06 Springfield. "Larger, smaller, or the same?" He didn't know, he said, because it was in a camouflage-patterned bag.

But it seemed that Alan had been promising gifts to the kids. He'd promised Molly a new iPhone and Seth a new mountain bike.

"And he and Mom are talking about taking us to Disney World during Christmas vacation," he said.

"I guess that's all good." I hoped my voice didn't reflect my irritation.

"But dad, I like my old bike."

I wondered if he was thoughtfully sparing my feelings or genuinely felt that way. I said, "Maybe if he gets you a new one it will have some features the old one doesn't. Or you could consider one a spare bike, in case the main one breaks down."

"I could. But I probably won't even use the new one." He paused for a moment, then in the same flat tone of voice continued, "He said he may be able to give me and Molly money for school clothes, too."

"Well, that'll be nice. Any idea how much and when?"

"No."

"I'm sure you'll both appreciate new clothes. Your mother should be able to buy you some things too." I wanted to add: Because I'm eating beans and spaghetti and living in a damn turd pit so as to send her a check every month.

"But I still don't like him. No matter what he gives me."

"Ah, buddy?"

"Yeah, dad?"

"Has he actually given you and your sister anything yet? I mean for gifts?"

He thought for a moment. "No, not really."

"So these are promises."

He nodded his head.

"Okay. Well, don't get your hopes up too high, bud, because sometimes we can't do all the things we'd like to do. Or even say we'll do. I haven't met this Alan yet, but it's possible he won't be able to follow through. Sounds like he's promising some things that'll cost quite a bit of money. So...what does Molly think about all this? About Alan."

"She likes him a lot. You know what she likes most?"

"No, what?"

"His car. She asked him to take her to the hair place two days ago because mom was working and you know what?"

"What?"

"When they got in front of the hair place...the, what do you call it?"

"Beauty parlor. Or hairdresser?"

"Yeah, that's it. When they stopped in front for her to get out, some of the other girls, Jeannie and Beth and I think April, were walking and she had him beep the horn. Three times."

"Why was that?"

"She said she wanted all the kids to see his car."

"Huh. So what kind of car is it?" I suddenly remembered Ralph saying it was a—

"It's a Corvette. A bright red one."

That night when I delivered Seth home I saw it in person, a flaming red Corvette parked in the driveway.

# 5

AS THE SUMMER wore on you didn't need to be an economist to recognize that the region was still in deep in recession. One always hears that Vermont is the last state to feel an economic downturn and the last to recover from it. There seemed to be truth to it. Vacant retail space; lightly-stocked store shelves; delivery and service vans showing rust; garage sales on every street; lawns cluttered with used cars, motorcycles and snow machines, all bearing "For Sale" signs— these told the story. People who'd never in the past driven a car more than three years old weren't trading. Others who'd always taken two-week-long vacations out West or maybe to Disney World, were settling for a weekend trip to the coast of Maine or were camping out closer to home at one of the many scenic, less expensive state parks.

Fine weather continued that week, the week after I'd met up with Ralph. So pleasant was it—and so low had my checking account balance dropped—that two consecutive mornings I gave up on the truck in favor of my bike for making job contacts. I figured I could at least get physical exercise from a work search fast becoming an exercise of a different sort, one in futility. It made no sense burning through ten dollars worth of gas going to a half-dozen businesses only to learn none of them was hiring or, in a few instances, were themselves laying off.

Ralph and I biked together a couple more days that week, taking the same eighteen mile route, much of it on paved roads, which were kinder to my skinny tires. He didn't complain but I knew he really preferred riding strictly the dirt roads or better yet, the rough terrain trails Collinsville had become famous for in the national biking magazines. Also, the hard-surfaced roads in and around the village aren't ideal for bicycling; even the state highway route has narrow shoulders with badly deteriorated pavement. Drivers don't generally slow down or swing wide either, and if you happen to cross over the white shoulder line there is always a risk of being struck by traffic.

When a near mishap occurred on Friday I didn't immediately view it as significant. We were riding along Route Two, past the Shell station and only yards from our upcoming right turn onto Verge Road, a well-packed dirt road which would eventually take us back into Collinsville. I'd heard the pick-up truck approaching behind me, had seen it in my tiny, handlebar-mounted mirror, and had steered as far to the right as possible without dropping onto the lower, rock-strewn gravel. I felt the blast of air as the truck roared past, a powerful, dust-laden burst of wind and then an equally powerful suction, like the vortex of a cyclone, which dragged me abruptly forward then crashing down, onto the graveled shoulder where I landed in a heap a foot or two beyond the bike.

Ralph, who had stopped a couple of minutes earlier to adjust his gear shift and was trailing by thirty yards or so, closed in on a jog with his bike. I'd gotten onto my feet, had taken my helmet off and was bending down to brush myself off—also to survey my skinned knees—when he bounded up, out of breath.

"Holy crap, Mark, are you all right?"

Straightening up, I coughed. "Yeah. I'll live." It wasn't the first time I'd had a close call but I knew this had to have been the nearest I'd come to disaster.

He set his bike down and removed his helmet. He looked pale as he turned, every line in his face drawn with concern. "Damn, I thought for sure—"

"Yeah, so did I. Guess I should have been further over." I rubbed at my face, over the bridge of my nose, which itched. Drawing my hand away I saw that my fingers were smeared with blood. I took a Kleenex out of the pocket of my shorts.

"I don't think so," he said. "That guy swerved toward you. I swear he did. He swung fairly wide by me but then he pulled over. Way over, when he got up to you. He swerved, Mark, I swear he did…Damn, you're cut."

"Yeah, hit pretty hard into the gravel. Did you notice what it was? What make?"

He winced. "It all happened so fast I…black pick-up…medium-sized Ford, maybe. The plate was…I don't think it was Vermont green. Could have been white with red numbers but I'm not sure. Sorry. Wish I'd paid more attention."

"No, that's okay."

"Guess I was more focused on how it was veering off toward you. Looked like he was going to hit you for sure."

"Didn't miss by much, considering the gust of wind."

Ralph was right. I knew my bike had been well over from the white shoulder line. It wasn't my fault, which meant—

"…and there's jokers who still say we don't need a cell phone law. Damn! The guy was probably on his cell phone. Maybe even texting." Ralph shook his head disgustedly. "Pretty bad when you risk getting killed just riding a bike."

"Yeah," I agreed, wincing at the tissue before tucking it back into my pocket. My mind wandered as I lifted my helmet into place and fastened the plastic catch. I wondered if the driver of the truck had been distracted by his cell phone or if he had swerved on purpose. I silently debated whether to tell Ralph about the previous incidents. They would certainly sound more credible now, in view of what had just happened, yet what was to be gained? Should I involve Ralph? I righted the bike; seeing no obvious damage, I sighed with relief. Of course, I thought, for his own safety perhaps I owed Ralph a full account: In case it was bad luck to be associating with me!

That day we ended our ride together at Ralph's place, a small, plain-looking ranch with a walkout basement in back, just off the state highway on Turner Road. He brought out a couple of cold ones and we sat on lawn chairs at the shadiest end of the long front deck. Through the screened window behind us I could hear the domestic murmurings of Ralph's brood, punctuated by an occasional clatter of cooking from somewhere beyond.

"You may not want to go riding with me again," I said, keeping the tone light.

"Why's that?"

"Because that near accident I just had was probably on purpose. That was the third close call in a month and a half. If there's another one I'd sure hate for you to get caught in the crossfire."

I'd gotten his attention; Ralph listened closely as I told him about the failed brakes and the salad dressing. He even held off from sipping his beer. I ended by saying, "All three have the same thing in common. They could have been on purpose or things that simply happened. I just don't know which."

"But who...?" Ralph left it hanging.

"Who. Why." I shrugged. "Again, I just don't know."

"You should tell Clem about today," Ralph said. "I'd be happy to back you up with a statement, too. I didn't imagine it. The guy definitely swerved toward you. I just wish I'd paid more attention to the truck."

"Thanks. I'll give it some thought. Trouble is, Clem didn't seem awfully interested before."

Julie came to the door just then and said it was time to eat. "Will you stay for supper, Mark?" she asked. "You haven't visited for a long time."

"Hi, Julie Thanks for the invite. I appreciate it but I really should be getting back." I got up from the chair, as did Ralph.

"Is that blood?" she asked, suddenly concerned, staring and then stepping onto the deck.

I took the Kleenex out again and rubbed it across my nose and daubed at my check. Not much fresh blood but quite a bit partially dried. I said, "And they say you never forget how to ride a bicycle!"

"You wait right there. I'll get a band-aid." She turned and disappeared into the house.

Getting a band-aid became much more: Julie emerged moments later armed with a wetted wash cloth, a towel, ointment and a box of bandages. She had me sit down again in the chair. "You must be sore all over," she said as she bent and set to work cleaning my wounds.

"No," I told her, "unless you count the soreness to my pride. Guess there's no band-aid for that!"

"Well, the worst here is the cut on your check. You only kind of skinned your nose. What happened, anyway?"

Looking over at Ralph, I warned him with squinted eyes and a slight twitch of my head not to mention what I'd just told him.

"Oops, does that hurt?"

"Ah, no. Sorry. Carelessness, Julie. Pure and simple carelessness. Narrow shoulder. Wobbly balance. When I heard the truck coming I should have pulled further over and stopped. Stupidity on my part."

"Actually could have been a lot worse," Ralph said.

She smoothed the large bandage out then pressed it with firm but delicate fingers to make it stick. I rather enjoyed the softness of her skin. The attention I was getting. "There," she said, "and the ointment is medicated so it should help keep out any infection."

"Thanks, Julie. Thanks very much," I said, getting up from the chair.

She started to turn, then added, "Are you sure I can't interest you in staying for supper? Nothing fancy, just pork chops, mashed potatoes with some vegetables from our garden. But there's plenty of it and—"

"Sounds delicious. Appreciate your asking, but I should be getting back. I've imposed enough with my medical needs."

"No imposition. I'm a nurses aide at work and a nurse here all the time with the kids. Hurt knees, elbows, you name it. Just call me Florence Nightingale!"

"Okay, Florence Nightingale it is. Thanks so much. Oh, guess I'll be seeing you again tomorrow at the rehab center?"

"Oh, for Asa. Yes! That's great, Mark! Ralph said you'd talk to the editor. Asa should get a big kick out of it. Just imagine, a hundred and two!"

"Yeah."

"Well, see you then." Before closing the door, she added, "Oh, it's right after lunch. Around twelve-thirty."

"I'll be there."

She paused and smiled broadly at me before closing the door.

Ralph said, "Back to what happened. I'll be happy to give a statement to Clem if it will help. That truck swerved, Mark, I know it did."

"Thanks, Ralph. I'll let you know. Keep you posted. Also about riding next week. Long range forecast looks good."

"Yeah. Looking forward to it. Talk to you later."

I carried that image of Julie—broadly smiling at the door—with me most of the bike ride back to my dingy apartment. I remembered years earlier when we'd first met, thinking she wasn't nearly as overweight as Ellen had earlier described; that although she probably weighed more than she would have liked or than was fashionable, any perceived excess was partially due to being so short, not much over five two or three. Unlike Ellen, who seemed to have consciously modeled herself after her damned Barbie Dolls, Julie's figure was that of a real, mature woman, rounded in all the right places. I remembered thinking that any plainness in her oval face or in her hair—straight, light brown and cut very short then, as now—was more than compensated for by that engaging smile.

Thinking of Julie, being reminded of how outgoing and genuinely friendly she was, I felt a renewal of that sense of disgust and shame I'd so often experienced whenever Ellen had talked about her. Early in our marriage I'd concluded that my now ex was likely an accomplished school-yard bully all through her elementary and high school years and that Julie probably had served as her primary target. I'll never understand why some people need to attack others in order to enhance their own self-esteem.

Al had told me the day before that when he'd sounded Maggie out over doing the Asa Warren story she'd sputtered. "Her exact words, Mark, were, 'Hell, no, those places give me the creeps. Especially that one. Besides, I never could stand the dirty old lecher.' So go for it," he said. "Two, three pictures—I'll run them. Maggie's known him for years. Says he was mean and horny as hell way into his eighties." He chuckled. "Maybe you can get a shot of him playing grab-ass with one of the nurses."

"Maybe."

That wasn't the way it worked out, however, when the birthday party for Mr. Warren rolled around the next day. For starters, the old man's butt-pinching days were clearly ended, although I suspected that had the flesh still been able the spirit would have been willing. He sat slumped, nearly motionless in a wheelchair, his shrunken, toothless head resembling a hybrid mix of vulture and Cabbage Patch Doll. His rheumy eyes did still shine with a dim glint of lustfulness and his grating, high-pitched voice remained strong, too strong at times as it frequently rang out in the small room in profanity-peppered staccato outbursts of command and complaint.

Ralph had dropped off little Carrie (then left, the coward!) for Julie to set up a five-generation tableau. The problem, of course, was she'd been unable to collect all five together. Asa's only living offspring, a daughter named Wanita, had declined to participate, citing health issues, and Julie's dad, she said, had told her he'd rather be the hooded guest before a firing squad.

"Do you think it's too much of a stretch?" she asked, cupping her hand in my direction so as to be heard over the chatter and commotion of staff squeezing into and out of the small room. I wondered why this event hadn't been staged in the large reception room or the dining room, but perhaps what seemed like a legion of well-wishers in the confined space would have amounted to a paltry few in a larger venue.

"Much of a stretch?" I repeated.

"Well, like, 'Missing from the picture due to unavoidable circumstances?'" she asked, gesturing a caption in the air with her hand.

"We could. It wouldn't have the same impact as...but sure, I'll speak to Al. He'll probably think of some way."

A couple of well-wishers left just then to make room for none other than Mr. Jeffrey Smith, the administrator. Julie discretely sidled away to resume her grip on the handles of her great-grandfather's wheelchair. Casting a patrician eye in my direction, Smith joined me where I stood toward a back corner.

"Reporting on the festivities, Mr. Sloan?" he asked, giving me a cold smile. Smith was tall, trim, ramrod straight, rather imposing in appearance with shocks of well-tamed, pure white hair and a handsome, uniformly tanned face surprisingly unlined for a man of perhaps sixty-five. Almost regal in bearing and manner, Smith seemed oddly incongruent with his fiefdom; out of place with the dingy walls, the harried bustle of nurse aides, the errant odors of un-emptied bedpans and disinfectant and bland, over-boiled vegetables.

I gave him one quick nod and said, "Remarkable, isn't it."

"You mean that we could manage to keep any of our residents alive that long?"

"I didn't say that."

"No, but...you see," he said, gesturing toward Mr. Warren, "wonderful things do happen here."

Just then, as though on cue, old Asa Warren's shrill voice rang out, something to the effect of, "Get away from me you f***ing, fat-assed bitch!"

If Smith grasped the irony of the moment he didn't let on. I fought off both a strong urge to laugh and a temptation, given his condescending manner, to continue our verbal sparing. Reminding myself it was Mr. Warren's occasion, however, I said, "Yes, wonderful things. We should be so lucky as to live that long."

"Yes, indeed, Mr. Sloan."

There was cake, distributed in small square pieces with white plastic forks on paper plates, and then an off-key group rendition of "Happy Birthday," which labored vainly toward spiritedness. Upon the fading of the final note Mr. Smith pointedly stared at his gold wrist watch (possibly a Rolex) and coughed. Within seconds the half-dozen staff still in attendance, with the exception of Julie and her daughter but including Mr. Smith as shepherd, had fled the tiny room.

Pictures were in order. While I adjusted my camera, Julie attempted to find the most favorable light, spinning Mr. Warren's wheelchair this way and that, back and forth like a portable stage prop. With every move and turn old Asa barked out another disagreeable, obscenity-laced command or sarcasm. (I wondered if Julie regretted having Carrie on the scene.) He had to be sponged off—judging by the cake crumbs and white frosting splattered over his face and pajama front, precious little of the cake had found its way into his mouth—and then cajoled by both of us into cooperating.

Just when it seemed the photo shoot was immanent, Carrie balked, refusing to get any closer than about four feet from old Asa. You couldn't blame her. By then I hoped Julie would give up on the generational theme and settle for a couple of shots each of her and Asa and Asa alone. But no. As though reading my thoughts, she said, "Carrie will thank me some day." In a harsher tone to her daughter she said, "Now you get over here right this minute, young lady! You're due a spanking if you don't!"

The end product of our efforts must have fallen well short of Julie's expectations. In every shot Asa Warren looked exactly like Asa Warren: an obstreperous, fossilized lecher. In one of the five generation-minus-two shots, little Carrie's face still glistened from her tears while in another she simply scowled at the camera; in all three she leaned so far away from Asa as to be nearly out of range. Julie looked frazzled in all the pictures, her hair a mess, her shoulders drooping and her mouth fixed in the same wan smile. Even she hadn't brought herself to cozy up to the old man.

The photos themselves told the story far better than any words I could string together but an article meant more money for me. Also, I knew that Al really liked playing up this sort of thing. It took me several hours, all evening and into the night in fact, to hammer out what I considered an acceptable feature article on Asa Warren. It required a fine balancing of elements: people who didn't know him might consider my treatment of him cruel; people who did might think me gullible, majorly sucked in. (Al liked my story. He phoned me after reading it Monday morning and said I'd be good at writing propaganda copy for the feds!)

I stopped by Harry's room after the birthday bash but found him sleeping soundly. A nurse aide urged me to wake him. "He doesn't get many family. I know he'd want you to."

I told her I'd plan to return within a few days."

"Mornings after ten are best," she advised. "They all kind of run down after lunch."

Made sense to me. So do I.

# 6

I DIDN'T LAND a job, even a part-time job, and in spite of trying to keep busy I found myself with more and more free time and less and less money to live on. Now, in mid-summer, there weren't many meetings to cover for the Banner, only one, in fact, that third week in July. Sorry to say, I sank into a despondent state of mind. (Probably mild to moderate depression, although I lacked the money or insurance coverage to pay for having it diagnosed, let alone treated, by an expert.)

I'd always believed that a person could get by on perseverance and hard work alone, that there was always work out there, that not finding it was simply an excuse for laziness. I'd assumed, without really analyzing it, that the folks lining up at the local food shelf were there mostly because they'd made bad decisions. Poor choices. Like my sister Charlotte, they'd acted unwisely, perhaps had more kids than they could afford to support, gotten into abusive relationships or spent too much on luxuries rather than necessities. As I was growing up, my parents' combined earnings placed our family well within the American middle class. I had taken financial security for granted. Even as an adult, my full-time carpentry earnings, particularly with overtime pay thrown in, were about comparable with what I could have expected in a typical profession requiring a college degree.

The rude awakening I experienced in mid-summer was painful, forcing me to reexamine some of my most cherished and long-held beliefs and, yes, prejudices. I'd played by the conventional rules and lost. Did it prove that perseverance and hard work weren't enough to succeed or had I simply made bad decisions, like the people losing their homes through foreclosure or those begging for food at the food give-away? I tried convincing myself that the reason or reasons for my dilemma were unimportant, that I should be focusing solely on how to dig myself out of trouble, but I needed to place blame and if I could chalk it up to rules changes then I could see myself as a victim rather than a poor decision-maker. The solution to rules changes was learning the new rules.

In the case of bad decision-making, well, I already knew that the biggest mistake I'd made was marrying Ellen. I guess deep down I knew it was a combination of both. The rules had changed because of the real-estate debacle, the over-supply of homes driven by the high rate of foreclosures, which had resulted in a record-breaking drop in home construction and remodeling. But I'd probably made some other mistakes too, aside from marrying Ellen. If we were still together I'd still be out of full-time work. Perhaps that detour into construction had been a mistake. With a degree in journalism, for example...

I toughed out the emotional roller coaster by alternately biking hard, three or four hours at a time each day (usually including an hour with Ralph), and then cooping myself up in my apartment where I would sit for as long or longer—often in the dark—brooding over the past, obsessing over things I'd done wrong or that others had done to me, and worrying about the future.

On one level I knew that indulging in such obsessive thoughts was unproductive as well as unhealthy, that I could be spending more time, for example, in widening my job search area. I tried forcing negativity away by focusing on things that were going well in my life. I thought of the kids; of my work on the Banner, which I enjoyed. I could take consolation in knowing there were several months remaining on my unemployment benefits claim, that although my income wasn't keeping up with expenses, I still had a balance-free credit card. I considered the fact that I hadn't experienced any further "accidents" after the biking incident with Ralph. That threat had evidently been one I'd simply imagined.

But negative thoughts are like parasites feeding on a host. Years of carpentry work had made me a carpenter. It was an integral part of my identity and I wasn't doing it. Not working full-time and not working at carpentry specifically seemed to be coloring every aspect of my life.

I fell into one especially destructive habit of repeatedly bicycling up Hudson Road so as to ride past the old Hudson place, nestled in its jewel-like setting of gnarly maples, fronted by a lush broad lawn created with the two hundred plus cubic yards of fill I had spent three years hand- digging and wheeling up from what became a full, finished basement.

I rationalized my taking that route again and again by telling myself I might see—be able to speak with—one or both of the kids if they were outside. In truth, however, I knew that at least Seth was unlikely to be home because Ellen had once again enrolled him in the activities program at the Collinsville Recreation Center. (Both kids were enrolled there each summer after they'd outgrown daycare but this summer Molly had outgrown that.) Nostalgia was the real reason. I loved that place which I had bought with my sweat. More accurately, perhaps, that place which had come to own me.

# 7

WE'D LOOKED AT a couple of other much smaller houses but Ellen had wanted to buy the Hudson place. Our wrangling over it had often grown heated. We agreed upon only one thing: The need for more space in which to live, ideally in a home of our own. With three year old Molly and Ellen pregnant with Seth, our tiny apartment above the health clinic on Main Street was uncomfortably cramped. I argued for a small starter home, something newer, easy to heat and not over three bedrooms in size. Something we could afford on my wages alone in the event that Ellen decided to stay at home with the kids longer than her maternity leave from her office manager job. Health insurance had to be considered. It wasn't available through my job with Todd so we were all covered under Ellen's policy at the company. We had to be able to swing a non-group, family health insurance premium along with a mortgage and all other household expenses on my income alone. Or so I believed.

Ellen saw the situation quite differently. She told me the Hudson house was "a steal" at the owner's asking price. "You didn't grow up here," she said, more than once, as though it were a capital offense, "so you have no idea how famous it is. Everybody here knows about the Hudson place."

She made sure I joined the "knowledgeable everybody" by recalling, ad nauseam, the things her grandmother (on Blanche's side) had told her about the Hudson place. How the wealthy Hudson family—in Blanche's mother's day they were the fourth or fifth generation of Hudsons to live there—had hosted lavish parties, inviting all the best people, hiring staff to tend bar and serve hors d'oeuvres, and occasionally even bringing in small bands to provide music for outdoor dancing on a large side terrace.

It was the Hudson family which, soon after the turn of the last century, purportedly bought the first motor car to ever be driven on Collinsville's then dirt streets. They were said to have been the first Collinsville family to buy a television set back in nineteen fifty-two. Over the years the Hudson children had attended private schools; nearly all had gone on to top colleges and universities and had left Vermont to pursue distinguished professional careers. In short, nothing about the family nor the home they had lived in had been drawn to modest scale.

"It was a showplace," Ellen said. "Even when I was a little girl it was still a showplace. I remember the last ones who lived there, an old white-haired couple. She always wore expensive looking wool tweed jackets with skirts, and with frilly blouses and fancy gold or silver pendants, sometimes with colorful scarfs. He always wore tweedy jackets, always with a tie. Even in the summer. I remember seeing them walk together down Main Street. Very...patrician-looking old couple. Maybe Collinsville's version of royalty." I hadn't liked the look in Ellen's eyes when she talked this way about the Hudson family or their now ramshackle, long-deserted home on Hudson Road.

The realtor showed us through the house once and then, at Ellen's insistence, a second time four days later. Our first time through I thought surely my wife would come to her senses; on our second I left in a state of shock.

The house obviously had been a showplace in its day, a large, two story, Adam-style colonial with a back-projecting wing; an ornate front entrance door with side lights and fanlight above; a wide, rather grand front hallway; six or more bedrooms (counting those in the wing); and inside chimneys at both ends of the main house supporting fireplaces on both floors. All of the original, period details had survived: the classic moldings and trim, the wide plank floors, the-six-over-six paned windows. Undoubtedly it had been a showplace. In its day.

As Ellen and the lady realtor babbled and gushed about such things as which room would be suitable for a nursery and what color drapes would look best in the enormous formal living room, I took thorough stock of the place. Todd did all of the cost estimates for his construction bids but even back then during my early years with him I had a pretty good head for figuring the cost of materials and the man-hours needed for specific projects. What I saw here boggled my mind.

The house hadn't been lived in for eighteen plus years and it certainly showed. In addition, only the kitchen and bathroom appeared to ever have been upgraded since the house was built in the early eighteen hundreds. What had spared it from deterioration by rot was its roof: someone along the way—presumably a Hudson—had roofed over the original wood shingles with corrugated metal roofing which, although uniformly rusted now, had protected the wood. A blessing from one perspective and from another a curse.

"You've told me a dozen times that the most important thing is the roof line," Ellen said at one point, "and just look at how straight it is."

She was right. At least about the straight roof lines on both the main house and the back wing.

"It starts with a straight roof ridge," I said in exasperation, "but it sure doesn't end there."

First, it had no basement, nor, by today's standards, a proper foundation. What it had was a cramped, dirt-floored pit, probably eight by six feet and no more than five and a half feet deep with walls of loosely stacked stones, which served as a cellar. The top course of stones supporting the sills were long, rough-cut granite blocks, dry-laid end-to-end and continuing on to form the sides of a shallow crawl space extending under the remainder of the house. This crawl space appeared to be no more than eighteen inches high as far back in three directions as I could see by flashlight.

The first floor ceilings were just over nine feet high. Incredibly, I could find no indication of insulation, either in the walls with tell-tale signs (in the horse-hair plaster inside or narrow clapboards outside) of fiberglassing or blown-in fill, or in the partially floored attic.

"The Hudsons you remembered living here," I said to Ellen when I later got to that item in my recitation of defects, "weren't simply making a fashion statement with their tweeds. Those folks were cold! They must have been half frozen eight months of the year."

"Very funny."

The hodgepodge of wiring was enough to send an electrical inspector over the edge; I'd never seen such a horrible mess! Every window needed to be replaced. All of the plumbing. Ditto the siding and the roofing. Water? Septic system? It probably had neither. My list of deficiencies went on and on. Everywhere I looked I saw a new problem, another dimension to the ever expanding pit into which we would throw our money if we made the dreadful mistake of buying the house.

Ellen's most insistent argument for buying the property centered on its low price. The house and small barn on twelve acres of dry, partially wooded land with seven hundred feet of road frontage carried a price tag of ninety-eight thousand dollars. (The Realtor said she thought the "motivated seller" might consider an offer of ninety-three.)

Ellen said: "We'd pay twice that for one of those junky little modular homes like...well, like Julie and Ralph Swartz have. Probably less than an acre, too, if it was anywhere near town. This is near town and has twelve. I call that a bargain."

"But we don't need that much land," I pointed out. "Not figuring the house or barn, that's eight thousand an acre. You can still buy a good two acre building lot for thirty. We'd be paying property taxes on ten acres we don't need." Underlying my reasoning, but not stating it, was the assumption that the house and barn would need to be razed.

Aside from the desirable price and the fact it had been the homestead of Collinsville's First Family, I could see only two real positives. First, the basic frame of the house probably was sound. Post and beam, I thought, and if the sills weren't rotted it could be salvaged, though at a tremendous and—in our position—prohibitive cost in time and money.

The other possible plus was the barn. During our first look at the property, toward the end of that cursory tour while I'd waited outside for Ellen and the Realtor to wrap it up and still believed we were wasting our time and effort, I had wandered over to look at the barn. I'd given it only a brief assessment, from the outside estimating it to be twenty-eight feet wide by about forty long and about fourteen feet up the side walls to the eaves. The walls began well above ground level, resting on what looked to be a substantial stone foundation. (I knew from Todd's occasional barn projects that those foundations were often laid up of larger rocks than those used under houses.) Although I had taken but a few steps inside before hearing the ladies emerge from the house, I did see that it was of post and beam construction which looked dry and sound. Given its condition inside and out, the barn was likely built some years after the house.

I never let on to Ellen that I'd seen potential in the barn because the last thing I wanted was to provide her with ammunition. At the time, however, I did think the barn could be rebuilt into a quite respectable workshop.

Blanche got into the act. My stock suddenly shot up. Until then she'd all but told me I wasn't good enough for her precious daughter but overnight I became the fastest, most talented craftsman she'd ever known. Just look at all the high-quality work I'd done on their house as a member of Todd's crew that year of the remodeling. The year I'd first met her, Harry, and then Ellen, home on break from college. She said if anyone could bring that old Hudson house back to its former showplace glory it was her talented, hard-working son-in-law, Mark. And when I'd finished we could host parties, just like the Hudsons had. One day she told us she'd had a brainstorm. "You two could start a bed and breakfast! It's big enough. With the ski area and all you'd make a fortune! Oh, and the bikers in the summer. Dear," she'd said in Ellen's direction, "I can just picture you as a hostess of a bed and breakfast!" ( I couldn't, nor could I picture myself as a genial host.)

Another hair-brained idea which Blanche ran up the flagpole about this same time was that I should quit working for Todd Drake and go into business for myself. I was easily worth ten (perhaps as much as twenty) dollars an hour more than I was getting, she said, and incidentally, did I realize he charged customers a "pretty penny" more per hour for my labor than he paid me, pocketing the rest? She was certain I could quickly build a construction business as large and successful as Harry's plumbing and heating business, at that point enabling me to have my legions of employees do all the work. She even talked to some of their friends, hers and Harry's, about potential work projects.

I spent hours working on the figures, taking every foreseeable expense into account for restoring the old Hudson house. In the end, even without adding the always necessary figure for unexpected expenses, my estimate of the materials' cost alone, excluding any contracted labor, was three hundred and forty-five thousand. When I presented Ellen with the total she brushed it aside. "We'll take out construction loans as we go along," she said. "The bank will loan us more as the house improves. Mark, it's a great investment."

Blanche said she and Harry wanted to do something for us. "Our money will all go to Ellen in the end but we'd like to see you enjoy some of it now." There was also an assumption on Blanche's and Ellen's part of a large cost-saving in that Harry's men could do all the required plumbing and heating free of charge.

I held out for as long as I could. I appealed to Harry, a mistake because it put him squarely in the middle. He sort of agreed with me. Said it would require a lot of money and years of labor, especially if I did much of the work myself. "Even," he said, "as fast as you work." He pointed out to Ellen that we'd be living in sawdust and dirt (with a new baby in a few months) no matter how careful I was. "Your mother complained constantly all the time they were doing over our house," he said, "and they always used drop cloths and vacuumed and sealed things off with construction plastic." (Of course we knew Blanche would have complained regardless of whether there had been dust.) But Harry couldn't be a strong ally for me. I understood that. I figured he'd fought the good fight with the redoubtable Blanche twenty-five years earlier, lost it probably within the first three, and had worked like a galley-slave ever since to keep up with her spending.

One mild evening over a beer on his back patio, out of earshot of Blanche, Ellen and little Molly, Harry recalled how he'd met Blanche. "It was at a dance," he said. "I was getting along then, you know. Not old but, what was I...thirty-two. Yeah, thirty-two. Most all my friends were married by then and had kids. I was already building up the business. Back then there weren't so many rules and regulations. It was a lot easier starting out. I hadn't dated much before I met Blanche so in some ways I was, well stupid when it came to women."

"How about wet behind the ears or naive? You've never been stupid."

"Well, thanks. Call it wet behind the ears, then. But anyway, when I met Blanche we just sort of clicked. She was pretty of course, but more important she was strong willed. I liked that. She spoke right up. Not wishy washy like some. Another thing was, we agreed on all the things that mattered. Like putting money aside and paying as we went. I was a real tight wad, you know, back then. Pretty rigid in a lot of ways but she didn't seem to mind, even agreed with me on most things. Best of all, she didn't look down on me. Some girls—women—acted like if you weren't a doctor or a lawyer you weren't worth anything. Just a plumber, you know what I mean? A plumber with dirty hands."

"Yeah," I said, giving a nod. I understood exactly what he meant except that his description of Blanche hardly matched with the Blanche I'd come to know as my spendthrift mother-in-law.

"No," he went on, looking off toward the lawn thoughtfully, "Blanche was different. She saw that I was a hard worker, had my own business. She didn't mind that I was a simple plumber..." Still looking off, he paused for a moment or two, apparently reflecting on that cherished memory of Blanche's acceptance.

I wondered where he was going with it. Also, whether he was blind to Blanche's obvious excesses.

"So," he resumed, taking a breath and looking back, "we went to a few movies after that, sometimes a dance, and then, I guess we'd been going together six or eight months, about that, when I asked and she said yes to marriage. Some people told me I was crazy. My sister, Dottie, for one. Called her a gold-digger. Not to her face, mind you, but Blanche knew what she thought. They've never gotten along because of it."

"Hmm...a gold-digger."

He nodded. "Yeah, as I said, I had a good business going, even as young as I was because I'd worked hard. Dottie and some others assumed Blanche was after my money. For one thing, probably by the way she dressed. She's always liked nice clothes. A sharp looking lady. Always has been. And yes, she can be uppity. She got that from her mother. They didn't have money but they were an old family here. Established. Take it from me, Blanche has never put on airs as bad as her mother did." He paused to sip from his can.

I followed his lead, raising my own Bud Lite. This was the first time Harry had ever talked to me as much about Blanche. I assumed he was doing it now to ease the hard feelings he knew I had toward her for so stridently advocating our buying the Hudson place. That was it, but Harry gave it an unexpected slant.

"Blanche means well, Mark," he said, lowering his beer. "I hope you see that." He studied my face for response.

"Sure, I know she does—"

"And it isn't all Blanche. Actually, this whole thing with the old Hudson house, a lot of it anyway, is my fault. Hers too, but I have to take my share of the blame."

"In what way, Harry?"

"Because if Ellen and I were closer I could reason with her. She might believe me when I say the place needs to be torn down. As it is, well, what does her old man know? We've never been as close as we could have been. Should of been. And that's my fault. I've always done nothing but work and make money. I wasn't there for her as much as I should have been. I know that now. Can't blame her mother for that. If anything, Blanche tried saving me."

That made no sense.

"Yeah, Mark, it's true," he said, my face apparently reflecting the question. "Saving me from myself."

"But if you hadn't worked so heard, Harry, Blanche wouldn't have all this." I turned slightly in the chair as I spoke and made a wide sweeping hand gesture toward the house. With a chuckle, I added, "And of course those marble countertops in the kitchen."

He smiled. "Sure," he said, "Blanche spends our money. Now that we have it to spend. She wasn't always that way, though. Not in the beginning, when I first met her. She's changed over the years. Gotten used to having it, I guess. Or maybe sees the real purpose of it. Money's supposed to make you happy, Mark. Instead of just socking it away it's supposed to be used. It's good to have enough but when you do, it's...time. Time," he said, underlining the word, "that's more important. Your time is where family and kids come into it. Where Ellen should have come into it for me. We had the money, Mark, I made sure of that. But what I didn't do was...was spend time with Ellen." His voice had taken on a low, dry tone in trailing off at the end.

He raised his can up to drink. He made it a slow, deliberate act, perhaps in keeping with his apparent remorse. Lowering it as slowly, he said, "Blanche tried. She used to want me to take time off. To do things for...well, just for fun as she'd say. She tried, in the beginning. As Ellen was coming up. 'Let's go over to Old Orchard Beach today' she'd say. It could be a Saturday or even a Sunday and I'd still beg off. Tell her she should take Ellen and go, that one of the crews had installed a new furnace and I needed to check out the work before billing. After a while she would go with Ellen. They'd go without me. As time went on she stopped asking. No," he said, shaking his head reflectively, "I can't blame Blanche."

Harry paused as we both heard the light footsteps, faint but growing closer.

"So anyway, Mark, I'm sorry for my part in all this. We both spoiled Ellen, I know that. And if I'd been a better father, not so wrapped up in my work, Ellen might be more willing to listen. As it is, my hands are tied. I just want you to know I'll do all I can. Blanche's hair-brained ideas only make things worse, which is a shame. But I haven't had any luck reasoning with her either and I don't expect to. It'll just have to work itself out." Little Molly appeared in the doorway; in a brighter voice Harry called out: "Over here, sweetie!"

I remember his words, remember equally well the tone of resignation in his voice. It had seemed to me then that if Harry had had a flare for analogy and a knowledge of drama, he might have likened our situation to that of characters in a Greek tragedy. We knew from the outset it would turn out badly for us; we knew it was inevitable that it turn out badly; and we knew there wasn't a damned thing any of us in the cast could do to prevent it from turning out badly because of our circumstances and the flaws in our character. Whatever lay ahead was inexorable.

Harry had given me many things to ponder in that frank discussion over a can of beer on his back patio. I understood most of what he'd said yet I continued to view him as a hapless victim of a bullying, spendthrift wife. His defense of Blanche only seemed to further ennoble him to me. I saw as heroic his taking blame for what clearly wasn't his fault. The comment about Blanche "saving him from himself" flew over my head entirely.

# 8

THOSE NEXT SIX years were a blur in my memory. Looking back I saw it as a miracle that I'd survived, that our marriage and young family had held together. Over the years since I'd learned to avoid discussing the details with people who didn't know me then. I had to be exaggerating. A braggart, maybe, feeding his sick ego? Nobody in his right mind hand digs an entire basement under a house using only a pick, a shovel and a wheelbarrow.

The first phase, remodeling the back wing to make it marginally livable, was the easiest and took only about nine months from the day of signing to complete. That section of the house had dropped a few inches and needed to be leveled with blocking and jack posts, work which I did, but I couldn't tackle a new foundation just then nor did I mess with the siding or roofing. I gutted the wing section, however, stripping it of plaster and lathe and then began restoration by installing new windows. Plumbing and wiring followed (Harry assigned one of his men to the plumbing; I did the wiring myself, with advisory help from an experienced friend) and then the insulation of the walls and attic joist cavities. One of the first-floor rooms—our future den—I sheathed with butternut wood paneling, reasonably priced through Todd. We contracted out the new septic and water systems (a dowser friend located a strong water vein eight feet down, two hundred feet behind the house) and Harry's man installed two small, temporary, vented propane furnaces for heat. We moved in that late fall, two and a half months after Seth's arrival.

Phase one had come off relatively smoothly. Ellen seemed happy with our new home, which already had over twice the amount of floor space as the apartment. I'd bought all of the building materials at cost through Todd; Harry had provided the plumbing and heating supplies and fixtures, refusing to bill us or turn over a list of what was used. Everyone was still on speaking terms.

I'd done nothing but work, of course. An eight—occasionally nine—hour day shift for Todd; a quick meal, then a six-hour shift doing the same type of work on our house, another light meal, shower, and then sleep. Eight to twelve hours of work each Saturday and Sunday. Same schedule, week after week, all summer long. No time for relaxation or television, no energy remaining for anything beyond work. As winter closed in I felt exhausted but happy. Meeting our first goal had been worth the sacrifice.

As I looked back over those years now I wondered how differently our future as a family might have evolved had the frenetic pace of reconstruction slowed with our moving into those first five rooms. If Ellen had been content to let me replace the roofing at a more leisurely pace the following summer and perhaps the siding during the summer after that. If she'd been willing to live in those five rooms— which were certainly adequate—for the next couple of years while we caught up on our bills and spent more quality time together as a young family.

I wondered and yet, looking back, I saw that I wasn't blameless for the way things actually turned out. Ellen hadn't stood over me with a whip those next five years as I'd resurrected the main house. She'd made it clear she wanted the house finished as soon as possible but as time went on it was my pride in the face of what seemed an insurmountable challenge which had driven me to obsessiveness and had rendered the old Hudson place my personal Mount Everest.

When well-meaning people, Harry and Todd among them, told me I was crazy to dig the entire basement by hand their words had had the opposite effect of strengthening my resolve to do just that. I couldn't blame them, however; what they said was true.

That first winter I gutted the main house. I began by carefully removing all of the old woodwork, all the ornate moldings, door and window trim, fireplace mantels, cornices, every piece which could be salvaged for reuse, and then I attacked the inside walls and ceilings, removing plaster and lathe creating great clouds of permeating, grey-white dust. It was not only the dirtiest work imaginable in the dead of winter, but bone-chillingly cold in rooms impossible to heat.

My incentive to persevere, which often flagged early on in the cold, grew stronger, however, as demolition work gradually revealed what was hidden underneath, when a magnificent superstructure of hand-hewn timbers emerged, morticed and tenoned together and held tightly in place with hand-carved wooden pegs, angle-braced at all the corners. From then on I stood in awe at the end of many work nights, filled with admiration for those skilled craftsmen of the past, often having to force myself to turn out the lights. My obsession with restoring the Hudson place had begun then, with discovery of those lovely, hand-hewn beams, wavy with grain, length-wise cracked and chipped smooth with adz; I had caressed them, tenderly run my fingers over them as though they were curving thighs and breasts and I was making love.

Ellen complained about the dust just as Harry had predicted. No matter how careful I was at sealing our living quarters off from the demolition, some dust always filtered through. "It isn't good for the kids. You wear a mask," she pointed out, "but we can't back here." I kept perfecting my techniques for sealing out dust but never got it right. My clothing was a problem. Wearing coveralls and work shoes and leaving them behind in the "disaster zone" didn't help; my body was so dirty each night after work that she continually criticized me for messing up "her" shower. Couldn't I figure out a way of hosing myself down before using "her" clean bathroom?

Harry often dropped by to check out my progress, always with beer to share and words of encouragement. I dreaded it when he brought Blanche: "Have you called that interior decorator yet?" she'd ask Ellen. "The one I told you about last week? You know, dear, that Greta somebody or rather who did such a marvelous job for the Murphys."

The next time she'd suggest where the sofa should be placed. "You folks will want one of those rich, dark brown leather sectionals with the built-in His and Hers recliners. That can go along here and then bend and divide this space up."

More than once Blanche decreed that we'd need a Jacuzzi "in every bathroom." Also a game room when I finished off the basement because, well, "all the better homes have game rooms." Except that we could be different and call ours a "billiard room" which would sound more sophisticated and of course necessitate buying a pool table. Marble countertops in the kitchen were assumed. Harry typically looked skyward on these occasions. What frightened me was that Ellen not only listened to her mother but would afterward comment to me that such and such a suggestion might be worth considering. "Mom does have good taste," she'd say, "and we do want a house we can be proud of."

Six years. It took six long, hard years to restore the old Hudson place to the point that we could be proud of it: four full baths, one half-bath, a finished basement— complete with "billiard room"—six bedrooms, a large formal dining room, an enormous living room (which Blanche often referred to as a "sitting room"), a den, and a kitchen worthy of feature in **Architectural Digest.** Except for the contracted work and Ellen's contribution of about an hour and a half of exterior painting on the front of the house, I had done it all. Although I wasn't privy to how much Harry had sunk into it, our construction loans combined totaled three hundred and eighty-five thousand dollars, which, added to the ninety-four thousand dollar initial price of the property, was the final amount upon which the monthly payments were based for our thirty-year, fixed-rate mortgage. I remember being sick on the day of the signing, having to use the rest room twice during our appointment at the bank. I also had a vivid memory of our drive home, that during it Ellen speculated about it being a perfect time to trade cars for something new.

# 9

BY LATE SUMMER, still working only the part-time job for Al and with my days relatively free, I was able to stop by the nursing home more frequently, three or four times in fact, during the last weeks in July and into August. I generally bicycled over to save on gas but took Seth along a couple of times in the truck. Harry still brightened up a bit with each visit. He knew me, I was certain of that, and knew Seth, but he was in obvious decline, noticeable from visit to visit.

One day I finally ran into Harry's sister, Dottie, over from her home in Burlington. I had met Dottie just once before, at Blanche's funeral, so had little to go on in forming a first-hand impression of her. I remembered Harry saying she'd been an Army nurse who had served in the Vietnam War, that she'd met her husband, Howard, at a field hospital there, that they'd lived and worked in Burlington for many years, and that after his early death she'd continued working as a nurse at a Burlington, Vermont hospital until retirement. From a disparaging remark Blanche once made about her sister-in-law, I'd gathered that in retirement, Dottie was somehow connected with a dog shelter.

I had also gathered from things Harry had said about her that his three-years-younger sister was a level-headed and practical woman, and that he, Harry, thought a great deal of her.

There was a facial resemblance between them: high check bones, a similarity in the squareness of their jaws. Also, in their eyes, not only in shape: In Harry's I had always read shrewdness, though shrewdness of a hybrid type, softened with warmheartedness; in Dottie's I saw shrewdness nearly unalloyed. A no-nonsense woman who could be as hard as nails if the situation warranted. Gray hair cut very short, tall, straight, mannish in manner and dress—I envied her plaid work shirt and black, cargo-style trousers—Dottie was clearly a Force.

Harry seemed to know us. Our combined efforts were even rewarded with the semblance of a smile. When Dottie bent over him he managed to mumble what sounded to her like "I love you." He was almost certainly "in there," trying to express himself, as we told one another minutes later, in the otherwise deserted lounge where we sat for a few moments to talk.

"I don't want to hold you up, Mark," she said, in a tone perceptibly deeper, more businesslike than it had been in the patient wing with Harry, "but I do want to thank you for checking in on Harry. I really appreciate it. For bringing the kids in too. The staff have mentioned it."

"I understand he gets a lot of visitors," I said, "but you and I and the kids are the only family."

"So I understand." She gave a knowing smirk.

I told her it was the least I could do, that as painful as it was watching him fail, I felt it was important for me to be there for him and for him to know the kids cared as well.

I guess with that, Dottie felt comfortable enough unloading on me. I had suspected most of it but hearing her vent helped me connect a few of the stray dots: how much she had disliked Blanche, how she'd rarely visited over the years because she'd always leave feeling sick over Blanche's "mistreatment" of Harry, how appalling it had been watching Ellen develop into a carbon copy of her mother. She covered it all, ending with how awful she'd felt when Harry had told her about our separation and then months later, about the divorce.

"But I understood, Mark," she said, nodding slowly. "I understood completely. You worked so hard and she used you. Just as Blanche used Harry. He dealt with it the best he could by immersing himself in the business. But he still paid a price for all that misery at home. I can't help but feel it was the stress building up all those years that brought on the stroke. Our parents both lived into their mid-nineties and so did our grandparents. Anyway, it's good that you're young enough to get on with your life. The kids will be luckier too, in the end."

"Maybe Seth. But Molly...I don't know about Molly." I left it at that.

We exchanged phone numbers. She asked me to please keep her informed as much as I could regarding Harry's condition. "I don't mean to burden you with it, but if you happen to notice he's significantly worse. They'll call me, I know, and...well, it only takes two and a half, three hours to drive over. But it's easier the more lead time I have. That's been the big problem, you know. Getting coverage at the shelter. I've got it set up as a non-profit now and can pay out a little on help if I have to but we're still on a shoe string. Donations and relying on volunteers."

I said, "I doubt he'll hang on much longer."

She agreed. "I'd like to be here with him at the end, if I'm able. Even if it's only to make sure they follow the DNR. But if it doesn't work out, so be it. Everything's set up anyway. The arrangements and all."

"You mean with...Ellen?"

"Good lord no!" She chuckled. "Heavens no! Harry gave me power of attorney just after Blanche died. Financial as well as health care. No, I made the arrangements here...write a check each month from his account. And of course renting the house. Well, dealing with the realtor anyway. They actually keep it rented." She paused for a moment, then smiled and added, "Harry knew better than to expect anything from Ellen."

It was also in early August, around the same time I was increasing my visits to the nursing home, that debate in Collinsville and neighboring villages between the pro and anti wind power project factions grew significantly more heated. I wrote a couple of articles for the Banner, one reporting on a petition drive to amend the town's zoning bylaws to prohibit industrial wind development and another covering a public informational meeting at which tempers flared so explosively that the moderator called in Clem McDonald and his deputy to restore order. Al printed both stories but for the first time ever, edited each of them slightly. A changed word or phrase here and there, in one a deleted sentence. I didn't mention it to him. His paper; his prerogative. The nature of the editing only added weight, however, to my impression that he preferred downplaying anything negative about loyal advertisers such as Roger Dornier.

I also hadn't dismissed the possibility that one of the Dornier clan, Roger or Little Don in particular, might have a motive for not welcoming my interest in digging into the more obscure details regarding the wind project. I plugged away at it, though, more out of curiosity to learn all the connections—perhaps even in the interest of self-preservation—than with any hope of using the information in an article which Al might edit or outright reject.

The proposed wind development project was complex. At that point, a permit was pending to allow erection of a test tower, the first phase in the process intended to determine feasibility of the site for wind power generation. Following approval, the test tower would then be built to collect data which the development corporation would use in its decision to either drop the proposed site or move ahead with the next phase.

New permits would then be needed from the State to allow for construction of the actual wind turbines, sixteen total, each one some 500 feet tall from the base to the highest arc of the blade. Securing approval for that final phase would present a great number of challenges, many relating to potential environmental impacts, including the possible effects of the project on soil and water quality; on human health, particularly on residents living within a one mile radius of the site; and the effects on wildlife, on bear habitat and the migration patterns of certain bird species.

Economic factors would also need to be assessed, including the number of temporary jobs provided during construction as well as the number of permanent jobs created to operate and service the huge wind turbines.

I'd heard or read that even that most basic question, at least to me, of whether there was a need for additional electric power, would be examined during the State's review of the proposal, although that issue always seemed to be raised as an after-thought, the implication being that "of course more power was needed. More power was always and would always be needed."

But opponents of industrial wind power development in Vermont, specifically, were pointing to the fact that more than enough "green" electricity to meet the State's full need was already available at a favorable rate from a Quebec, Canada, hydroelectric source. Why, then, they were asking, was there need for an additional source?

One aspect of the proposal seldom mentioned by proponents, except tangentially to stress the need for expeditiousness in both the State review process and commencement of construction, was the generous—but possibly soon-to-expire—federal government incentive subsidy paid to developers/owners of wind generation facilities in the form of Production Tax Credits, amounting to 2.3 cents per kilowatt hour of electricity supplied to the national energy grid, for a period of ten years. A further incentive for electric utilities buying the power was profit through sale of Renewable Energy Credits, or "green tags," used by other utilities to offset their use of fossil-fuel-generated power, enabling compliance with federal carbon emissions standards.

When this issue of subsidies was raised with the corporation's chief spokesperson at the informational meeting I covered for the Banner, he scoffed, and, in a demeaning voice said: "Well, folks, obviously there have to be incentives!" It was as though any fool should know that! Wind power wasn't competitive yet with hydro and fossil fuel, he continued, but "progressive, visionary thinking" required looking at the larger picture. Required looking at "dwindling fossil fuel reserves, at the catastrophic effects of global warming due to burning them, and at the urgent need for transitioning to renewable, nonpolluting energy sources."

One soft-spoken, seemingly knowledgeable gentleman at the meeting said he'd done a "comprehensive cost-benefit analysis" of industrial wind and found that on balance the negative consequences, environmental as well as financial, greatly outweighed the positive benefits. "This," he said in measured tones, "is all being driven by politics, profit, and the mistaken notion that it will be good for the environment."

Perhaps to allay negative public reaction without actually taking a firm stand, two members of Collinsville's three-member Select Board told me following the meeting that concern over the project was premature because the developer might abandon the plan altogether given the long, drawn-out process ahead. In guarded terms, they led me to believe they leaned toward opposing the project, citing in particular the importance of preserving the natural, unspoiled beauty of the land. Days later in a radio interview, however, one of them stressed its positive aspects. A case of wanting it both ways, it seemed to me, pointing to the potential economic benefits regionally and to the country as a whole as we transition to renewable energy while acknowledging—in person to an audience of highly vocal, very angry townspeople—that the wind turbines would scar the ridge line forever, diminishing the bucolic splendor made iconic in countless calendar photographs of scenic Vermont and attracting tourists from around the world.

Most credible observers believed the project would sail quickly through the State's permitting process, unchanged and in its entirety, due to the strong backing of Vermont's environmentally conscious Governor. Also due to the fact that members of the State's Public Service Board were appointed by the Governor.

# 10

HARRY'S CONDITION HADN'T deteriorated significantly enough to alert Dottie when I stopped by the nursing home again at the end of that same week but while I was in his room I kept hearing a commotion in the room next to his. As I stepped into the hallway to leave I learned that a Mr. Dubie had died moments earlier. I heard mention that calls were being placed to nearest of kin—apparently none of whom had made the scene—and that a funeral director had been summoned to remove the body. By the liberal shedding of tears by nursing staff, I gathered Mr. Dubie had been a favorite patient.

When Julie suddenly appeared in the doorway, eyes red, checks glistening with tears, I realized I'd lingered too long, that it was too late to simply duck out. Seconds later, bending a bit, I was providing a handy shoulder to cry on as well as embracing arms in a consoling hug. She clung to me tightly for what seemed like minutes, between gasps declaring what a wonderful, kind, thoughtful man he was.

I hated myself for the awful thoughts, but as I stood there just beyond the threshold of death, the warm feel of Julie in my arms stirred more in me than sympathy. I suppose our tight embrace might have lasted longer than even she intended.

That Saturday night, without knowing why he'd asked me to be there, I found myself sitting on a stool next to Todd on the bar side of one of Collinsville's four restaurants, the one most commonly frequented by budget-conscious locals. Ben was there also, drinking Coke due to his age, but talking with a couple of younger friends at the other end of the bar when Todd finally got around to what he had on his mind.

"I kind of wanted to keep you up on the latest," he said, stroking his beard. I'd sensed by his upbeat mood he had good news. "No guarantees. And if I get it, it'll be damned cold by the time it's closed in for finishing. Anyway, I mailed a bid out on a pretty good job yesterday morning. Condos up on the mountain. Twelve units. You know that big lot just to the right of the lower lift?"

"Yeah," I nodded.

"Well, that's the site."

"Wow! Nice going!"

"As I say, I might not get it. Might be high. I figured it close, though, so if I don't get it, whoever does isn't going to make any money." He raised his glass stein to drink.

"Damn! That's great, Todd. Hey, I'm happy for you!"

"The thing is," he said, setting his beer down, "I know you're writing a lot for Al. Good stuff too. I keep up. Looks like you're full time, or near it." He posed it as a question.

I shook my head. "Nowhere near. Mostly nights, covering meetings. No, I've still been looking. Nothing much out there." I paused, then, "So if you get it?"

"No guarantee, as I say, but if it comes through, we're going to have to bust butt. We'll need help, Mark," he said, turning to face me, "yours, if you're free. All winter, probably half the summer finishing up with just the three of us. I'm hoping things will get back to normal by then so we get more work. I assumed you'd still be interested but, well, just wanted to make sure. In case you had another offer or something."

I felt my throat tighten with emotion. "I ah...thanks, Todd. I don't know what...hey, I appreciate it. Just say the word." I chuckled and added, "That is if I'm still in good enough shape to swing a hammer!"

He had no idea how appreciative I felt. Well, maybe he did. Minutes earlier he'd told me he'd put a second mortgage on his house a month ago to keep his head above water.

Todd's good news changed everything. As if by magic, by the waving of a wand, I felt relieved of an oppressive burden. The dimly lit bar suddenly seemed brighter; the background babble—a too-loud cacophony of raucous voices and laughter—had grown less irritating, even agreeably pleasant. I raised the heavy beer glass, clear and amber, and thought perhaps...but dismissed it. Only my second Miller. Tame as beer goes. No, it was Todd's news which had raised my spirits. I'm a carpenter; this was a possibility of returning to work!

I've never been one to spend hours in a bar. Even during those lonely nights following the breakup of our marriage. Even when I'd had to leave the kids and the house I'd put my heart and soul into restoring, I hadn't reverted to drinking, either in bars or alone in the sorry-ass dump I called home. That night, however, I stayed until nearly closing. Todd and I caught up, first at the bar, and then—when Ben joined us after his friends left—at a table. It was reminiscent of our old end-of-the-week bull-banter session, sans the tail-gate.

At one point, as he often did, Todd asked about Harry. I filled him in, told him about meeting Dottie, the fact that she couldn't get over as often as she wanted, that I visited when I could, but...

Todd said he felt bad he hadn't visited him since going there once, in late winter. "I always liked Harry," he said, looking down, "and he sure sent a lot of work our way over the years. Damn! I kick myself. Maybe I'll plan to—"

"No, don't feel bad," I said. "Hard telling how much actually registers. He did manage a slight smile yesterday. Dottie thought she got a whisper out of him but he can't talk. Sometimes I wonder if it's harder on him having people he knows come in and not being able to talk. It's got to be frustrating, anyway. Very sad."

"Sure is. Ellen ever...?"

I shook my head. Reaching for the glass, I said, "Apparently not. Not to my knowledge, anyway. Haven't run into her there nor has Dottie."

"Too busy with her social life. They make quite the scene at all the night spots, or so I hear. Party panthers. I wouldn't know first hand. I'm usually in bed by nine-thirty."

I sipped, then set the glass down. "They? You mean she and Alan, what's his name... " Three beers and a Freudian block on his last name.

"Yes, Alan...I don't remem—"

"Ames." It was Ben, who'd said very little after joining us.

"Yeah, that's it. Alan Ames.," Todd said. "His sister's the one who works in the lawyers' office, the one in Ed Holt's block next to the hardware store. Husband was in the guards, the bunch they sent to Afghanistan. Remember the guy who got killed?...stepped on an IED?"

I did, but vaguely, and nodded.

"He's the one. Bad scene. Couple of kids and they'd just bought that place out on Route Two. Anyway, this guy, this Alan, is her brother. Moved in with her a few months ago. Has a bunch of used cars for sale out on her front lawn."

"And pickups," Ben added. "He had an S-10 a month ago but it was a rust bucket. Plus, he won't dicker."

"How come you know so much?" Todd asked, turning.

"I get around, old man, I get around!" Ben said, reaching over, giving his father a playful punch in the shoulder.

"I don't want to know how much," Todd said to him. "Anyway, he sells them. Guess he's taken over one of the two bays of her garage, turned it into a shop. Fixing minor stuff, brakes, mufflers."

"Smelled like he was spray painting the day I stopped," Ben interjected. "Door was open and he had a mask on."

"Probably does some auto body too. Anyway, I guess they've both had bad luck," Todd continued to me. "I heard he had a car accident. Injured his back. Supposedly limited in what he can do for work but that doesn't mean squat, as we all know. Apparently got some insurance money out of it...of course. Don't they always?"

"They seem to," I said. "Okay, that all jibes with what my kids say. The latest is, he's moved in with them. With Ellen. Lock stock and barrel. Must be a month, month and a half now, since they told me. I don't know anything about him except that he's been making promises about buying stuff. Bikes, clothes, iPhones. Planning a trip to Disney World. Last I knew he hadn't followed through, which is fine with me. I don't want him giving my kids anything. But I'm wondering if the guy's nothing but a bull shit artist."

Todd said, "That's kind of what I've heard."

"Nice Vett he's got, though," Ben commented.

I agreed. "Nicest thing parked in that driveway in the last twenty years," I added.

Before the evening was out, somebody—Ben I think—mentioned the proposed wind development. Todd complimented me on my reporting of it. "You're thorough, that's for sure. Don't know that I understand it all." He paused, then added: "That last meeting must have been a rip-snorter. Glad I missed it."

"Oh yeah." I went on, said it was a complicated issue and hard to cover, that some people wanted it that way. "Little Don Dornier, for instance. Well, and Roger, too, who spoke up in support of his brother."

"Do they still speak to you? I heard you've upset both of them big time."

I said Roger had been avoiding me since our face-to-face confrontation over the gun debate, and that I'd heard Little Don wasn't happy with me. "I haven't run into him, though, since the article. We all figured he was at least part owner of the land on the summit," I continued, "but apparently we weren't supposed to know he has a major interest in the company itself. I suspect he has a couple of friends on the Public Service Board too, but I may not be able to prove it. And even if he does...nothing illegal, I guess, unless I can find business connections."

Todd nodded. "Right. A small state like this. Bound to be hidden ties here and there. Obviously, Roger isn't speaking to me. Hasn't since the court settlement."

Todd had suddenly jogged my memory. It all came back in a rush: the lawsuit he'd been forced to file against Roger after we'd built his gun shop and he'd refused to pay the cost overrun due to all his changes to the original plans. Todd had won the case and, as I recalled, there'd been such hard feelings, he'd doubted he'd ever get another job from a member of the Dornier family.

"...but I couldn't get Clem to spend any time looking into it," Todd was saying, "you remember...the ax job on my truck tires?"

"Oh, yeah." Another prod to the memory. It was fall. We were up to our earlobes in work. Todd went out that morning to get into his Dodge Ram and discovered all four of the new Michelin snow treads—mounted two days earlier—had been savagely ruined by some ax-wielding lowlife.

"I thought it was more than coincidence," Todd said. "Roger ordered by the judge to pay me the twenty-four grand he owed. Then my truck tires slashed, all the same week. Funny thing though. Clem doubted the two could be connected. Told me I was imagining things."

"Well," I said, still remembering back, "wasn't Roger a problem from the git-go? Seems to me you had trouble with the Zoning Board even before you started. Didn't they close us down for a few days because he hadn't gotten his permit?"

"Hell yes! I'd forgotten." He looked at Ben and continued, "Son-of-a-bitch lied and told me he had all his permits. Raised holy hell when they said he'd be paying a fine...remember how much?" he asked, turning to me.

I said, "Damned, I don't. Not exactly, but it was hundreds a day."

"It didn't take long to get one, though," he continued. "Dad stepped in. They waived the posting of a notice. No thirty-day waiting period. Then, bingo, like magic, we were back on the job!"

It was late. I'd had maybe one beer too many. The last thing I needed was a DWI. If I'd been reminded earlier of Todd's run-in with Roger, the lawsuit and especially the tire slashing, I'd have gotten into the business about my biking mishap. I'd shared the failed brake incident while still working with them; also my suspicion about the salad dressing and Clem's ho-hum response. If there'd been time to update Todd and Ben, two people other than Ralph would have known. They might have heard or seen something bearing on what happened. Perhaps offered advice.

On my drive home, however, this regret was overshadowed by my excitement over the possibility of returning to work.

# 11

THE FOLLOWING MONDAY at around 9:30 in the morning, I got a call from Julie. Her voice over my cheap cell phone sounded muffled, as though she was holding her phone a long way from her mouth. At first, not hearing clearly and believing it was a telemarketer, I nearly clicked off.

"It's Julie," she said, not much louder than before, "Julie Swartz. Can you stop over?"

"You mean at the nursing home? Is Harry worse? Or ...?"

"No, I'm at home. Our place. I didn't go...to work...because..." There was a long pause, then she said, "Can you possibly stop over? I hate to bother you, Mark, but..." She trailed off to an even weaker sound, a soft gasping, as though short of breath, which became outright sobbing.

"I'll be right there, Julie. I'm coming."

My mind raced through all the possibilities as I locked up and ran for the pickup. Was she hurt? Was Ralph? One of the kids? Was there an intruder?

She met me at the door. In the split second before she thrust herself into my arms, I caught her look of anguish, a red face streaming with tears.

"What is it, Julie? What's happened?" I said in alarm.

Between gasps: "He's left us...Ralph...he's...he's... gone...last week. On Thursday...he didn't come home... all weekend...he's... he's..."

I patted her back gently for a minute or two, then released my grip, intending to separate from the embrace, but I felt her arms tightening and for several seconds we stood, awkwardly enfolded, just inside the door.

Finally, she stepped away. "I'm sorry, Mark," she said, softly, her red eyes shifted down, "I didn't have anybody else to talk to and last week you were so...well, with Mr. Dubie and all, I mean..."

She dabbed at her eyes with a handkerchief, then invited me into the living room where we sat, awkwardly at first, as she continued to composed herself. She'd taken the two youngest girls to daycare and the oldest to the summer program as usual, she said, but then had changed her mind about going to work. "I didn't think I could face it today, so I called in sick." She'd also left work a couple of hours early on Friday, she added, "Right after you were there. It wasn't just Mr. Dubie dying. It was Ralph, too. I've been upset like this ever since he left last Thursday. Just can't seem to think straight."

I shook my head slowly, put on a sympathetic face, said it was all a shame and being upset was totally understandable.

Would I like a cup of coffee?

I did. Likely my first big mistake of the morning. No, make that the second. My first was answering the phone.

"...so we've been fighting over it a long time," she said minutes later, setting a cup of steaming black coffee down on a coaster on the glass-topped coffee table in front of the sofa where I sat. "Milk? Sugar?"

"Just a little milk, please. Thanks."

"It wasn't any good, I mean having the girls hear it all." She sat down with a cup of her own, sat very close, in a stuffed chair next to and at a slight angle to the couch. "Every time I've brought the subject up, it's only to be supportive, Mark. I swear. I say, 'Maybe you could try this or that. So and so needs help, maybe they'll hire you.' Then he lashes out at me. Says I'm nagging. I don't understand. I've never been unemployed."

"Well, take it from me, it isn't easy being unemployed," I said, in mild defense of Ralph. "I know how helpless he feels."

"Yes, I'm sure you do. But look how you've handled it. You haven't let it get you down. You didn't throw up your hands and stop trying. You didn't think carpentry was the only thing you could do."

"Well no, but... "

"'Delivery driving is all I've ever done.' That's been his stock line, over and over, from the beginning. 'It's all I know how to do. Delivery driving.' I've gotten so sick of hearing it I could scream. I keep saying 'there's dozens of things you could do to earn money, Ralph. You just have to believe in yourself. Try something different. So what if it's something you've never done before. That doesn't mean you can't learn. Yes, you could fail. Yes it could be a dead end. But at least get out there and hustle. Get off your ass and try.' Excuse my French."

"It's rough on your self esteem, though, I went through it and—"

"Sure, it is, Mark. I know it is! I'm not saying it isn't. It's just that when you have a family to raise and bills to pay you have to get over it. Sitting around feeling sorry for yourself doesn't cut it. Probably the last thing I ever wanted was a job toileting old folks in a nursing home. But it was all there was out there. Back a few months ago when I thought the girls were old enough for me to get a job. We were barely making ends meet on what he made, Mark. With two girls in school it was getting harder and harder. School clothes, supplies, braces, all those things. It wasn't easy in the beginning, either. I had to take the LNA course. But I did it. I did what I had to do and so could Ralph."

"Well, I see your point, Julie. But the longer you go without working, the harder and harder it is to feel positive about yourself. It isn't something you can just switch on. I mean—"

"Oh, I know! How well I know. But...heck," she said, with an apparently urgent thought, "I almost forgot this part! Two weeks ago there was a janitorial opening at the home. A temporary one, anyway, to fill in for old Mr. Forrest. Old Martin. He took a bad fall, ended up with a broken arm and some ribs and can't work for at least eight weeks. I saw the posting on the board. First thing I said to Ralph that night: 'The job could be yours for the taking.' You think he'd check it out. Oh, no! What do I hear? 'But I don't know anything about janitorial work.' So I go: 'It says no experience required. I've watched him. He pushes a broom around. Buffs the tile floors, dusts and vacuums. What's to know?' So what do I get? 'But it's only temporary. If I take it I can't be out looking for a permanent job. It wouldn't be good to quit without two weeks notice.' Yada, yada, yada. Name the excuse and he throws it at me. I've gotten so tired of hearing it!"

"Well, I do sort of see your point."

"The same with part-time jobs! No, no! Of course we can't be looking for one of those either. Not to support this family. 'But Ralph,' I go, 'part-time is better than nothing. It would add at least a little bit to our income. To your unemployment check. And who knows, some part-time jobs become full-time.'"

She paused for a moment, turned to give me a smug, self-satisfied sort of smile, then went on: "Oh, yeah, what really got his goat was when I used you as an example! I said 'Ralph, 'you need to take lessons from Mark. He hasn't come up with one lame excuse after another for not hustling.'"

"That couldn't have been very helpful, Julie."

"Well, I've wanted him to think about what a real man does when he's faced with a challenge. Just look at the facts. You've done carpentry all your life. Right? So I'm guessing you want to go back with Todd. Isn't that right? Or if you can't, you want to get a carpentry job with some other contractor. Am I right?"

"Um...yes," I said, nodding.

"So what do you do? You go to work as a newspaper reporter, something I'll bet you'd never done or probably ever considered doing. Not just that, but it's only part-time. Right? Part-time work. That's what I said to Ralph. 'Look at Mark. Mark's a perfect example of what I'm talking about.'"

"But there's a difference," I said, aware of her leaning further and further toward me, "in a way, I mean. I don't have to earn quite as much as Ralph. Yes, I'm paying child support, sure, but my apartment's cheap and I don't have a lot of other expenses and... " I felt her hand touching my shoulder, then gently rubbing it.

"You don't need to make excuses for Ralph," she said. "I know what Ralph is. He's a loser."

"Julie, you shouldn't put him down that way. I mean—"

"He is, Mark! It's true. Look at him! He's a complete loser! It hasn't been easy all these years. Half the time I don't get an ounce of respect. He didn't really want girls, you know, so what do we have? Three girls. Do you think he has much to do with them? Heck no! I'm practically raising them alone. He doesn't lift a finger where the girls are concerned. No, he wanted sons and I know he blames me for not having one. Just think of how selfish that is! I have to do most of the work raising our girls because I didn't give him the son he wanted. Isn't that ridiculous!" She paused for a second, then went on, "And now to run off and leave me alone with them, it's just... cowardly, that's what it is. Cowardly! You're twice the man he is, Mark. And you want to know something else?"

I gulped. "Ah...what's that?"

"I think Ellen's a fool."

"Ah...a fool?"

"For letting you go."

"Ah, Julie, I think we'd better—"

"I hated her, you know," she said, looking away philosophically. "Yes sir, I hated Ellen with a passion. What she did. They call it bullying today but back then in school we never heard it called that. She badgered me about everything. My weight. My height. I was shorter than most girls and even in junior high, Ellen was quite tall. Tall, slender, and good looking. I was always conscious of being overweight… couldn't seem to lose, no matter how hard I tried. My clothes were mostly hand-me-downs from my sister. Clean and mended. My mother made sure of that. But old and worn. Dowdy, really. My hair usually a mess. I'd try getting away from Ellen…oh how I'd try! But there she'd be. Flaunting a new outfit or a different hair style. Always rubbing in that her parents had lots of money when she knew mine didn't. Always dressed in new outfits, the latest and best. Always the fashion queen, you know, even in graded school but especially when we got to high school. Her mom would take her to Burlington to clothes shop. Once or twice to Boston, even, just to buy the best and latest."

"I'm sorry, Julie. I kind of thought that from some things she said, but—"

"Oh, and the cheerleading! I'd forgotten about the cheerleading! I didn't really want to be a cheerleader but my mom said why not try out for it? So I did. Big mistake, I'm telling you! I did everything but fall flat on my face! Not a graceful bone in my body. Worst experience of all. You'd better believe Ellen flaunted that in my face when she made the cheerleading team! She had a natural talent for it, you know? Always showing off, I mean. That and the dancing lessons made her a natural."

"I know it must have hurt you a lot, Julie, and I'm sorry. Girls can be cruel. I'm sure being bullied can effect you right into adulthood."

"Well, in one way Ellen didn't let up even after school. She had everything going for her from kindergarten on. Then, you know what?" she asked, facing me from the side. "After college she got you."

"Got me? You mean…?"

"Married you. I'm serious. Do you know how bad I felt? How it all came back…all the old hurt, when she introduced us? Yup, I thought, Ellen's scored again."

"Why would you— "

"Because I knew that first time I met you that Ellen was still getting the best of everything. That I'd have to settle for seconds or thirds like always before. It was like the bullying had never stopped. She was still proving herself superior, this time with you as the prize and me settling for ...well, let's face it, Ralph wasn't any prize catch. Don't you see," she said, her voice softening, becoming tender, "that in a way we're both victims? Victims of Ellen?"

She paused. In the silence, I sensed her leaning toward me, closer and closer. Then I felt her hand, resting again on my shoulder, warm and still for a moment and then moving slowly, first in a gentle stroking motion, back and forth across my right shoulder blade. Then onto my neck, her fingers lightly messaging up and down for a few seconds, continuing around and finally rubbing with longer, gentle stokes across my upper back. She had slid up from her chair, was now sitting on the arm of the sofa. "That's exactly it," she said, in a whispered breath, at my ear. "Don't you see? We have that in common, Mark. We're both victims of Ellen. How about you and me getting even with both of them."

We kissed. Long. Intensely. What she did next, and after that, required no words.

Did I know what was about to happen? Oh yeah. I wasn't born yesterday.

Did I do anything to prevent it from happening? No. But I wasn't up for sainthood. It had been over two years—no, make that closer to three, including the nights I'd slept in a guest room in my own home—since I'd enjoyed the pleasure of sex with a woman. Celibacy sucks!

Besides, doesn't a gentleman do as much as he can to aid a damsel in distress?

Julie was good. Sweet in passion and skillful. If this was getting even with Ralph, she gave it all she had and I, obliging in kind, was a fortunate beneficiary of her vengeance.

Afterward, while tidying up the living room—we hadn't in a literal sense violated the marriage bed—she told me Ralph had been the first, that she'd never done it with any other man but had always been curious.

I couldn't tell whether or not I had satisfied her curiosity; whether I had pleased or disappointed. (Couldn't any deficiency on my part be attributed to lack of recent practice?) In fact a bit of awkwardness had crept in between us as we kissed and said goodbye. As I looked back, however, to see her standing in the doorway, she flashed that smile—that broad, womanly, engaging smile which transformed any plainness into beauty.

# 12

I KNEW BETTER than to expect word from Todd that week. It occurred to me it could take a month, even longer, before a decision might be made on his bid. Then there was no guarantee he'd land the job. The initial excitement and hope I'd felt at the bar Friday night was waining.

There was also the sobering fact that if Todd's bid won we'd be framing into late December and still sheathing the sidewalls, setting the trusses and closing in the roof late through the coldest, toughest portion of the winter. Outdoor building construction in Vermont normally ends in early winter due to the often brutal cold and heavy snowfall. Todd always tries planning it so he has a house or two framed and buttoned in with heat and ready for inside work to last through until spring. If he did get the job it could mean working under some quite difficult conditions; in spite of it, however, I wanted in the worst way to get back to full-time construction work.

With the cash flow situation growing critical I resorted to using my credit card, even for routine expenses such as groceries and gas, knowing full well the high interest charge and the danger of spiraling deeply into debt.

Tuesday night, the day after I'd stopped by to "comfort" Julie, I had an especially hard time getting to sleep, mostly due to worry over how I was going to continue to eat and pay the bills. (Regret over having sex with Julie probably figured into it also. After all, I was an adult, no longer a hormone-driven teenager bent on scoring. I should have left when Julie came on to me. A married woman, married to a friend.) I tossed and turned, thinking of the rent coming due again soon, thinking of the check I'd mailed that afternoon for the six-month premium on my truck insurance, a check all but draining my account. What were my options? I was someone who'd always taken pains to assure that I had them and here I was, down to a meager few dollars, forced to tap my credit card, running up a bill at an exorbitantly high interest rate with no firm prospect of being able to soon pay it back.

I'd been brought up to believe that borrowing money and spending on credit were generally a reckless practice, often a prelude to financial ruin. It's an old-fashioned notion in this age of easy, instant credit, a conviction shared by few people of any age today. I trace it back to two sources, the first being my parents.

My dad, born only two years after the 1929 stock market crash, rarely discussed his childhood and adolescence but I know that he grew up in poverty. His father, an alcoholic, had worked at a series of low paying jobs, always for a few weeks or months at most before being laid off or fired. His mother had also worked at odd jobs, supplementing their sporadic, meager income. There were no anti-poverty programs. The family had lived hand-to-mouth, moving often, evicted from one rat-infested apartment to another all the years that dad and his brother were growing up. I understood that when he was old enough to leave home, my father had resolved to make a clean break, to leave it all behind and make a better life for himself. He'd succeeded—even later loosing track of his "deadbeat" (his term) brother—mainly by serving a hitch in the U.S. Army during the Korean War (although not sent to Korea) and afterward going through college on the GI bill. He'd put the past safely to rest but the lessons from it had been indelibly stamped in his psyche, strongly enough that he'd managed to instill them in me, perhaps his greatest legacy. He never preached the importance of fiscal responsibility to me directly; he demonstrated it by living it.

My parents were both older than those of most of my friends. They'd met in college, both majoring in education, aiming for degrees and certification to teach school. Due to his first having served in the military, my father was five years older than mom. Following graduation, they'd both found good teaching jobs and soon afterward had gotten married. It was another two years before my sister Charlotte was born—Charlotte who, unlike me, was planned for rather than conceived by accident (some thirteen years later). Judging by the number of photo albums devoted to my sister, I gather she was doted on from day one. Perhaps even more than Ellen was because I suspect that unlike Harry, who came from a family not quite as down and out, our father wanted Charlotte to have all the advantages denied to him.

Charlotte: by negative example, the second source of my firm belief in the virtue of avoiding debt. I was at an especially impressionable age when, due to a series of appallingly poor decisions, Charlotte's life spiraled out of control. Early pregnancy, a succession of low-wage jobs, abusive relationships, two failed marriages, several more children—I believe a total of five by multiple partners—and years of dependence on welfare. Our parents repeatedly bailed her out whenever she appealed for money; during one low point they even took in two of her youngest kids, temporarily sparing them from foster care ordered by the state. (Although the connections between stress and disease aren't yet fully understood, I'll wager that the years of anxiety over Charlotte, added to the stress of his work, caused or at least contributed to our father having developed cancer.)

I worried over my lack of options late into that Tuesday night. No prospect for additional work. No guarantee that Todd's bid would be accepted. No family to turn to except my seventy-six year old widowed mother—something my pride would never allow unless the alternative was sleeping on a park bench. Also hardly a viable option given that she lived nearly two hundred miles away in a tiny one bed-room apartment on a fixed income. (And was likely drained already of any spare resources by my profligate sibling!)

The next day I had a comeuppance of sorts when I groused to Al about the high interest rate on my credit card. He agreed that banks were charging usurious rates, that they needed to be reigned in. Then he unexpectedly stood up, took out his billfold and asked me how much money I needed.

"I can't take your money, Al," I said.

"Call it an advance on your pay. Or a loan. I'm certainly not going to charge you interest."

With sincere thanks, I turned him down.

Just as I was leaving, had in fact pushed the door open, he motioned for me to stay, saying, "Do you have another couple of min-utes, Mark?"

"Sure." I closed the door.

"Please," he said, indicating the chair, then continued, "I wish I could offer you more hours, Mark, I honestly do. But there's only so much—"

"Hey, I know, Al. I know you do and I appreciate it." I could feel my throat tightening. One of those moments when words stop coming. When pride struggles with gratitude. That along with a suspicion of pity as the root of munificence.

"But there's only so much news to cover out there. Meetings. Issues. We're doing a great job covering it all. And I think the balance between news and features is just about right."

I gave him a nod.

"So what I've been thinking about lately is something else, some other way to make it worth your while to stay."

"To stay?" I said, finding my voice and leveling eyes with him across the desk.

"Well, yes. Here at the paper, naturally. But also in the area. I know you're having a hard time making ends meet and you're hoping to get back on full-time with Todd. I also don't see the economy improving any time soon. It isn't all bleak. There are signs of it happening nationally. But as we all know it takes awhile to filter down. Anyway, you haven't said but I'm assuming you're looking outside the area. I mean for work." It was a question posing as a statement.

"Well, no, I—"

"Because I would be. I wouldn't blame you if you were thinking of moving. South, maybe. Maybe out west. With winter coming on and all. And no jobs around here. That's what I'd be thinking, anyway." His eyes were steady and inquiring, his brows knit to intensity.

"Ah..." he'd caught me off guard. The thought hadn't occurred to me. I said, quickly, "No, Al. Never would leave on account of the kids." I heard the strength of determination in my own voice. "I may be forced to commute further for a job but leaving the area isn't an option." I paused. Hoping to inject a note of levity to lighten the mood, I smiled and added, "Sorry, but I'm afraid you're stuck with me for the foreseeable future."

It did break the tension as Al also smiled and said, "I'm certainly not feeling stuck, Mark. Far from it, believe me." His face growing serious again, he hesitated for a moment as though debating how to go on, then said, "So that brings me to something I'd like to run by you."

"Shoot."

He paused, then said, "I'm wondering if you'd be agreeable to taking a share in the paper's profit. Call it a...oh, a bonus." He stopped for a second, glanced away, then back. "No, it would really be a share of the profit. We'd base it on a percentage of the net for the year, with an advance on it now when you can really use it. Would you accept that?"

Again a tightening in my throat...my mind rapidly reviewing assumptions. First that Al subsidized the Banner and therefore there could be little to no profit to share. Second, that this was merely a relabeling of his earlier offer of a pay advance or a loan. I felt a renewal of that just-passed mix of emotions, that tangle of gratitude and mild hurt from a perceived poke at my pride.

"No, Al," I said, "I can't take money that I haven't earned. I've never done it and won't begin now. I really appreciate the offer, though, I do. Things aren't desperate. Nowhere near it. Thanks, but I'll get by."

Al often seems capable of reading my mind. Either that or I never manage to prevent my face from acting it out. He said, "Don't get me wrong. I'm not offering you charity, Mark. This isn't personal, it's purely a business matter." His voice carried a note of brusqueness.

"I didn't mean that it was. But the paper can't be doing so well that—"

"Hey," he said, holding up a protesting hand, "that's my department. I wouldn't be making the offer if I didn't think it could." He paused, took a breath and in a more thoughtful tone, continued, "You've probably noticed that we've picked up some New Hampshire advertisers lately. A few, anyway, which will boost revenue. I haven't crossed the river much. Aggressively, I mean, because we'd need to extend news coverage for that. But I've targeted the ones who draw customers from over here due mostly to the sales tax."

"Yeah, I've noticed. The Harley dealer for one."

He nodded. "Right, the biggest ad from them. A couple of others, too, and I'm expecting to hear back from a stove dealer." He paused for a second. "But the other positive thing is circulation. It's way up. And there's only one reason for it, at least that I can see. That's having you on the staff. Your reporting."

"No Al, that can't be—"

"No, wait," he said assertively, holding his hand up again. "Hear me out. This will be the best year yet for the paper. It's already showing in the figures. I'm not blowing smoke, Mark, or making the offer out of pity. The paper's gaining in ad receipts and circulation, mostly do to your work here. You're doing a great job and I'd hate to lose you. Even if Todd can hire you back or you find something else full-time in the area, I hope you'll stay on here."

Stunned as much by the earnestness in Al's voice as by the words themselves, I know I simply stared at him for several seconds, unable to respond. Then, finding my voice, I told him I would. With regard to his offer of profit sharing, I told him I'd feel best if we revisited it at tax time. That in January or February he'd know exactly how well the Banner had done for the year. We left it that way.

On the street outside I felt a strange combination of emotions, a mix of elation over Al's obviously sincere appreciation for my work, but also a sense of shame over not having graciously accepted it. Why did I automatically protest when he'd praised my work, saying I was valued as a reporter for the Banner? Why did I continually put my self down? Was all my self-respect gone, drained due to a few personal challenges, none of which was close to being serious?

As I reflected, I suddenly saw for the first time one factor which had undoubtedly contributed to my tattered self-esteem: Molly's hurtful comments. It didn't occur to me in the context of placing blame—I couldn't blame Molly, she merely echoed her mother in putting me down. No, I had only myself to blame, namely for allowing Ellen's values to continue to define me. Why did I think of myself as desperate? Because in Ellen's world, that's where I surely had to be. My apartment had to be a bed-bug infested dump. I didn't have a full-time job so I had to be a shiftless bum. We might be divorced but I was still allowing Ellen to define who I was, granting her power over my self-image, letting her chip away at my self-esteem. I felt ashamed in realizing it. I hadn't been true to my own values, the same ones Harry had lived by, or tried to. The same values, in fact, which I was hoping would be instilled in Seth. I felt ashamed of myself for allowing it to happen and decided it had to end.

Al did his best to give me more hours over the next two days of that week, asking me to sell advertising both mornings, letting me cover a routine meeting in person that Thursday night rather than relying on secretaries' minutes, and assigning me a human interest feature story to cover Friday afternoon, one he would normally have given to Maggie. (He said she'd be just as happy letting me cover it.)

Early on I'd often felt guilty taking work away from Maggie, thinking she probably needed the money. Not only the money but also the challenge, the satisfaction, the shear joy she derived from doing it. Sometimes I'd hear her whistling on her way through the door of the office, sometimes bursting in, full of excitement over a dramatic "scoop." She took real pride in always getting the facts straight and in following as strictly as possible the inverted pyramid structure so Al could cut anywhere below the first couple of paragraphs if necessary. Perhaps most important, she kept her own opinions and judgements out of her news stories, painstakingly avoiding subjective wording which might taint the straightforward reporting of objective facts.

For months I'd worried about horning in on Maggie but that had recently changed. She and Al probably hadn't expected anyone to be entering the office only three minutes until closing time that late afternoon when I stopped. At first I thought the office was deserted. No one answered when I called out at the front desk; the door to the inner sanctum—the paste-up room—was closed, a rarity. The voice I heard bidding me to wait was so muffled I couldn't tell which one of them had spoken. They were a full five minutes coming to the door, both red-faced and looking somewhat disheveled. Hey, both adults, presumably consenting.

One of the regular advertisers Al asked me to visit that week was Roger Dornier at his gun shop. I hesitated before agreeing, thinking the less I had to do with any of the Dornier clan the better. But Al was doing his very best to give me extra work, which I appreciated, and being desperate for the few additional bucks it would net, I agreed to make the contact.

I've never liked any of the Dornier boys. A burly bunch of obnoxious red-necks as far as I'm concerned. Their father, Donald, has a sort of down-home, rustic charm which makes him likable to an extent, but I've heard from many sources that he drops the charm during business dealings, becoming ruthless in getting what he wants on his own terms. Of his four sons, Little Don and Roger take after him the most with respect to his business prowess, and Keith (my landlord) and Wade, the youngest, although increasingly proving themselves capable in business, also seem to have inherited a bit more of their father's personal charm. I suppose what I find objectionable about them, particularly in Little Don and Roger, is that air of superiority. A touch of entitlement, perhaps. Exaggerated self-confidence, probably rooted in having dad behind them and not yet having experienced any sort of failure. One can't call any of them bad but all four could be improved by being knocked down a peg or two.

It probably wasn't a good idea, but on my bike ride to the gun shop I recalled and brooded again over those memories of Todd's troubles with Roger. It had all come back vividly Saturday night in the bar, our being told by the zoning administrator to cease and desist just as we were framing the walls, hearing Roger brow-beat the poor town official before he could escape—calling him every vile name in the book for simply doing his job—and then, when we got the go-ahead to resume construction, putting up with Roger's strutting around and loudmouth gloating over how much power he and his dad had in "setting the god-damn town straight."

I recalled that Roger and I had begun locking horns all the way back then, probably from the time he'd learned that I was born and brought up in Massachusetts—a "flatlander" in the local parlance—and when, instead of ignoring his bluster, I had argued with him as I'd worked. Todd let him blow off steam without comment but between hammer swings and power saw cuts I told him zoning laws were necessary and needed to be enforced. He argued back, his face growing red above and even through his shaggy red beard. Said I was full of shit, that a man's land was his to do with as he pleased and nobody had a right to tell him what he could or couldn't do with it. He wouldn't back down nor would I.

The next time Roger stopped by the work site the issue we got into was gun control. He railed against having to run even the minimal record check, mandated on all customers purchasing guns. (Under the law, if the federal authorities didn't respond within a certain brief time period, the gun sale could go through.) The Second Amendment to the Constitution guaranteed the right to bear arms, he said, and that was that. It was none of the government's "god-damned business" to restrict that right in any way.

I countered that for many people that was fine, that I owned a rifle myself, but that felons and the mentally deranged, for example, shouldn't be allowed to own them. I said the lack of restrictions in many states, including Vermont, was enabling mass shootings, domestic gun violence and street killings on a daily basis across America.

Todd stayed out of it although I knew he mostly agreed with me. He never told me to stop baiting Roger, probably because I didn't pause from my work to argue with him. One afternoon as we were picking up our tools to go home, however, he did ask me if I enjoyed our verbal sparing.

"Not especially," I said, "but I'll be damned if I'll let him get away with thinking I agree with all his redneck crap."

Shaking his head, he'd told me Roger was "one of those people who needs a two by four 'side the head to knock any sense into him."

I remembered again that Todd couldn't get all his money until taking Roger to court; then there was the tire slashing incident. I should have known better than to be recalling all of this now as I entered his gun shop because it undoubtedly influenced my disposition.

The polite young man at the counter asked my name, ducked briefly into an adjacent room, then returned saying Mr. Dornier would be right out.

Mr. Dornier did come right out.

It didn't begin well nor did it end well. Roger acknowledged me with a gruff, "It's you is it." Before I could explain why I was there he informed me he'd been meaning to tell me how "f*****-up" my reporting on the wind project was. "There's a hell of a lot of people here who think this thing's a good idea. You made out like everybody at the meeting was against it and against Donny. That isn't true and you know it."

"I reported what I saw and heard, Roger. I guess we'll have to agree to disagree on this one."

"And writing it up that Donny's in the company...that's none of anybody's god-damned business!"

"Al thought it was. He left it in the story. Now the reason I'm here is—"

"I already set Al straight. I'm just telling you you don't need to go poking your frigging nose into what's none of your god-damn business."

"As I said, we'll have to agree to disagree. I think the public has a right to know all the facts. I can't say I'm going to quit going after them...But why I stopped by, Roger, is to—"

"Tell you the truth, I couldn't give a rat's ass why you stopped by," he said, glaring over the counter. "I'm guessing Al sent you 'cause of my ad. It's his day. So how's about you hotfooting it on back to him and telling him to come in himself."

Bad enough leaving the gun shop with my tail between my legs in failure. Worse yet having to flee down the road on a bicycle. A rusted, sadly outdated bike at that.

# 13

THE SECOND WEEK in August marked the end of the summer break for elementary and secondary kids in the Collinsville school district; school reopened on the following Tuesday. Now, every other weekend—provided Ellen cooperated and the stars were aligned— I would hear a recap of the goings on at school rather than at the recreation center's summer program. It would be mostly sixth grade news because as the summer had worn on, Molly had either left Seth and me before the weekend was out, or, most recently, had refused to come at all with Seth. Sorry to say, but over time, after enduring an endless string of complaints, put-downs and biting sarcasm, I'd lost all patience with her. I didn't want her around, poisoning the atmosphere and lately she had obliged.

Thankfully, Seth was untainted by all his sister's drama, still a joy to be with. I admired his constitution but worried over the attitude he could be forming toward the opposite sex. My concern was probably wasted because he'd talked as much about the girls at the recreation program as his male friends.

Thursday evening of that first week of school, I called Ellen to set up a plan for the upcoming weekend.

"Molly won't be going," she announced in a triumphant voice. "She doesn't want to and I'm not about to make her."

I told her that was fine. Asked her to please put Seth on the phone. During the minute or two it took him to answer, I mapped out a plan I thought might work. When he came on, I suggested we might go fishing on Saturday. "How about it?"

"Fishing? Sure dad. Where?"

"Oh, let's see..." I paused, making a kind of game of it, as usual, as though we had thousands of bodies of water to choose from, but knowing I would say Tyler Pond, our favorite spot and the place we always went. "How about Tyler Pond?"

"Tyler Pond? Sure. Sounds great, dad."

"I have your pole here and I think your creel. I'll pick us up some crawlers at the store tomorrow. Be good if we could get a really early start Saturday morning. Suppose your mother will let you come over tomorrow night? Sleep over here?"

"Maybe right after school?"

"Sure, If she'll let you."

"I could take bus three," he said, "like I did that other time, and walk up the hill."

Before answering, I thought of what he had for clothes in the apartment. His boots were here...a light jacket... "Sure, you could, if there's nothing you'll need from home. Oh damned," I said, remembering.

"What dad?"

"Oh nothing serious, bud. I just have to cover a meeting in the afternoon. It won't be done before you get off the bus."

"No prob, dad. I'll take my key."

"Oh, that's right. I gave you a key to the palace." I could hear his nervous laugh. "Okay, buddy, but I'll hold while you check with your mother."

He came back on within a few seconds and informed me she had approved. As always happened under those circumstances, I switched off the phone feeling smaller. My son, yet I had to grovel. I wanted there to be a time of reckoning, a single moment when all the hurt could find release. Even a single moment when the scale could tilt in my favor.

It worked out as it was supposed to. The Planning Commission met at three—apparently one member of the all volunteer Commission worked on an evening shift—and I got back to the apartment at four-thirty. Seth had let himself in with his key and was watching TV when I arrived. On the way home I'd picked up a fairly decent, well balanced meal for us from the deli. We ate, watched TV and then, before turning in for the night, switched to one of the DVDs he'd brought from home, another of his fantasy films featuring super heroes and evil giants committing horrible acts of mayhem and destruction. I don't know how a kid can sleep soundly after watching all that violence but I guess it's nothing new. Many of the bedtime fairy tales our mothers read to us were no less gruesome.

Thanks to Seth having stayed over the night before we did get an early start to Saturday. We loaded the canoe on the pick-up, packed some sandwiches and soft drinks for lunch, gathered up the poles and creel, remembered the crawlers from the refrigerator, and were out at the pond by a quarter after seven, on the water ten minutes later.

Tyler Pond was as scenic as ever it could be, just then greeting a rising sun with mirror-calm water and only light wisps of misty fog remaining and quickly dispersing in the gathering warmth. We heard birds, lots of birds chirping in the trees along the shore and spotted what looked to Seth like an eagle swoop down from overhead into a clump of birches. "Except it could a been something else," he said.

Our lines in the water, we rested the poles at an angle against the gunnel. I heard about the start of school. Same classmates plus three new ones, he said. He'd already made friends with one new boy and there was a new girl he'd sat next to at lunch yesterday and was hoping he'd get to know better. A new homeroom teacher who sounded as though she wouldn't be tolerating any fooling around, and a "goofy" math teacher he thought he'd get along with a lot. Bullying was evidently being made a big issue.

"Nobody's bullied you, right?" I asked.

"Oh, no." He shook his head vigorously. "They're saying it with Molly, too."

"You mean at high school?"

He nodded. "Mom got a letter."

Oh geez! It figured. "A letter saying...what?" I kept the tone casual.

"About bullying."

"You mean bullying in general? Not about Molly?"

He thought for a moment. "I think its in general."

"Was Mom upset?"

"No. And Molly said she didn't."

"Didn't bully?"

"Right. That she didn't do it."

No point in quizzing Seth. No point in even knowing whether his sister was in trouble for bullying because Ellen wouldn't be approachable on the subject, let alone allow me any input into what should be done about it. If Molly treated any of her school mates the way she treated me I could easily imagine someone accusing her of bullying.

The fish weren't biting. Maybe because we were talking too much, too loudly? Oh well, catching fish wasn't our primary purpose for being there, at least not mine: every moment I could spend with Seth was precious, regardless of what we were doing as long as we were doing it together.

Naturally we talked about Harry. Seth led off, saying, "I sure wish Grandpa Harry was here. He'd love it."

Funny, but he had echoed my thought exactly and at the exact moment.

"Yeah, buddy. But do you know something? You know what I think?"

"What, dad."

"Well, we both know that Grandpa Harry can't be very happy where he is now. Right?"

"Right."

"And we both know that he won't have to be there all that much longer, right?"

He nodded.

"So you know what I think? I think that when he gets to that better place it'll include being here at Tyler Pond. That maybe next summer when we come here fishing we'll feel like Grandpa Harry's here with us."

"Looking down from heaven?"

"Well, something like that, yes. We can't say for sure how it works, but I'm thinking it will. So we can feel sad over it now but happy, too, can't we? Looking forward to his spirit being with us, maybe next year?"

"I hope so."

"So do I, buddy."

It had been two full weeks since I'd had Seth with me, since the weekend he'd told me about Alan's promises of a new bike for him, a new iPhone for Molly, new school clothes and the possibility of a trip to Disney World at Christmas. I wanted in the worst way for him to bring up the subject himself, wanted to hear if any of the promises had been kept. The longer he avoided the subject, or seemed to, the more my anxiety grew. What if Mr. Ames had followed through and the iPhone and bicycle had arrived?

Admittedly, I had felt hurt over the whole thing. Damn sore, in fact, over a perfect stranger moving into my kids' home and promising them things I couldn't possibly afford to buy for them myself. Of course I wanted to hear from Seth that the promises hadn't been kept. That Alan hadn't produced a bicycle or an iPhone or money for school clothes and that there wouldn't be a trip to Disney World. Not so that I could gloat over it or put the guy down. It wasn't in me to do that. But so that I could feel my son's respect for me wasn't slipping away. Sad to say I had allowed him such power, but Mr. Ames' encroachment into my kids' lives had begun to tarnish my self-image as a father, and here I was, needing assurance that my unconditional love for my son was enough.

As it turned out, my fears were unfounded. Seth got into it when I asked a general question about how things were going at home. Everything was going fine, he said, then following it up with, "...and Alan hasn't given me the new bike yet. I don't want him to either." He seemed relieved.

"Ah...Molly's iPhone?"

He shook his head. "Not yet," he said. "But do you know what Molly wants now, Dad?" he asked.

"I can't imagine," I said, suppressing a strong urge to roll my eyes.

"A car."

"Good heavens!"

He nodded.

"But she isn't anywhere near old enough to drive a car."

"She's fifteen, dad. She can get a learner's permit so she wants her own car."

I had trouble grasping it. Fifteen? Molly, driving? I said, "So she's asked Alan for one?"

"Yup, and he said he'll look out for a good one to give her."

"Hum. Well, lucky Molly. I guess." I heard the dry strain in my own voice. Maybe because that was one promise he might manage to keep.

On Monday afternoon, quite by chance when I stopped into the office to speak with Al about assignments for the week, it was Maggie who fleshed-out—from a decidedly feminine perspective—my vague mental picture of Alan Ames. By then I had seen the immaculate, older model red Corvette on the streets of Collinsville, presumably being driven by him, but I hadn't yet seen enough of the driver to take stock of his appearance.

As part of Al's project to put together his special annual, four-page insert devoted to Collinsville businesses, he'd given both Maggie and me the names of four or five relatively new area businesses and asked us to interview the owners and write up a brief description of each business, taking a picture or two of interest on each site. This was something he'd done from the beginning; the little boost in public awareness of new businesses had paid off in that most had continued to regularly advertise in the Banner. The insert would honor—by prominently listing—more established businesses as well, especially those which consistently placed ads.

It seemed that two weeks earlier Mr. Ames had cut out, completed and mailed in with a check, the ad order form regularly printed in the advertising section of every issue. He'd submitted a small sketch of a car, specified the type-styles and font sizes for the ad, designing it so well that Al hadn't needed to contact him but instead, had simply composed the ad as per Mr. Ames' instructions. Even though it was a small ad and, as Al said, "The guy's probably a fly-by-nighter like most of them," he'd put Mr. Ames on Maggie's list of new businesses to feature in the insert. (If I'd only known I might have asked her to switch with one of mine. It was high time I met Mr. Ames.)

I was sitting in the one chair in front of Al's desk, talking with him when the door opened and Maggie "floated" in, seemingly on some sort of ethereal cloud. Al slipped his glasses off and set them on his desk.

"God, but that's a handsome man!" she panted. Her smile, as giddy and foolish as I'd even seen Maggie wear, lit up the tiny room.

Relinquishing the chair as she drifted toward it, I stood next to Al's desk.

"Charming to boot…and those bedroom eyes…oooh," she said, waving her hand in a fanning motion in front of her face as she sat down.

Al said, "Get a grip, Maggie, you're hyperventilating."

"So I am."

"Which member of our species inspired this rapture?" I asked, adding toward Al, "Sort of like watching a Christian swoon at the second coming!"

"That new used car guy," she said quickly, then turning toward Al, "It's all your fault, you bastard, for sending me out there!"

Al shrugged. "Hey, just a name. I haven't met him yet."

"Let me guess," I said. "A Mr. Alan Ames?"

Maggie's deeply lined face suddenly flushed. "Oh no! Sorry hon. I've heard the rumor and—"

"More than a rumor and yeah, I know where he got his bedroom eyes today. But like Al, I haven't met him yet either. So he's good looking and charming, huh?"

"Well...yes," she said, regaining her composure.

"So did you discuss his business at all or just gawk at him," Al asked, obviously in good humor.

"Or swoon?" I said.

"I have enough to go on, don't worry."

"And what, maybe a picture you can sell to Play-Girl Magazine?" Al quipped.

"You guys are just jealous, that's all! No," she continued, growing more serious, "he has great plans for expanding. Not there necessarily, because it's his sister's place, but somewhere in the area and down the road. Build up a business and in time take on a franchise for some line of new cars. He bent my ears for a good hour. He is a charmer, as I say—"

"I believe more than once," Al cut in.

" ...and he talks a good line but...okay, I'll admit it guys, I have my doubts. I think a lot of it's only pie in the sky."

Squinting, with a look of skepticism, Al said, "Ya think?"

"Earth to Maggie! Earth to Maggie!" I couldn't resist.

"Okay, guys, have your fun. No fool like an old fool. And yes, even an old girl can fantasize. Okay, so what do I really think? Aside from the charm, the great looks and the bod to match? A mile-long line of bull shit and, as they say, flat broke without a pot to pee in or window to throw it through."

"Exception taken, Maggie," I said. "I've personally contributed both the pot and the window!"

That broke them both up.

"I don't know your ex very well," Maggie said, "but I'm surprised she's let him move in. Date him, sure. Fun for awhile but I doubt he's the kind of guy you'd want to depend on for the long term. Guess I'm saying I'd have given her more credit."

I agreed. "Especially if he's broke. Only one thing motivates my ex and that's money."

"Apparently that isn't all, hon. At least for the time being." She paused, then said in a cautious, tentative tone, "I don't mean to pry into your business, Mark, but... well, I wonder if she's thought about...well the influence on your kids."

I told her it bothered me as well. "My only hope," I added, "is that it won't last long. For all her faults, though, I know Ellen wouldn't do anything to jeopardize the welfare of the kids."

"So does it sound like he's doing any business?" Al asked.

"He said he's sold quite a few this summer, including a couple of pick-ups. The cars look good, the half dozen or so he's got out there by the road. He said they were all trucked up from Florida, never been exposed to salt. Bought them at auction down in Mass. He's fixed over one side of the garage into a shop. Does some auto body work if they need it. Spray painting dings and so forth. Not very good at it, incidentally. My son Harold's been in the auto body business for what..." she paused to consider, "hell, it's been close to thirty years, now. So I know a professional job when I see it. This guy's work is... um...maybe on a par with what Harold did as a sophomore in high school auto mechanics. Looks good until you get up close."

"So he's planning to expand?" Al asked.

She nodded. "As I said, he told me this is only temporary until he gets on his feet and can buy a piece of land of his own. Someplace with the same visibility but where he can put up a three or four bay shop with an office and sales room."

"I take it he isn't ready to place a full-page ad," Al remarked, dryly.

"Ah, no." She paused for a moment, then said, "I did compliment him on the fine job he did in designing his ad. I told him it fit perfectly into the one column space. He said he had previous experience working in a print shop."

# 14

I BICYCLED TUESDAY afternoon, missing Ralph's company in that it had seemed easier maintaining a brisk, steady pace biking with him and I'd enjoyed our conversations. In another way, however, I knew it would be hard even running into him, let alone biking with him. Sure, I felt bad over what had happened. Remorseful. I liked Ralph. We'd once been fairly close friends and a rekindling of that friendship had been well underway. A friend doesn't treat a friend by having sexual relations with his wife, however. Ralph would likely never know—Julie said it was our "safe little secret"—but things of that nature often come back to bite you. What women swear they'll do or not do and what they actually do are often two different things. Come to that, it isn't only women!

It was likely inevitable that my circuitous route that afternoon would include a ride past a certain used car lot beyond the Shell station out on Route Two. I slowed down as I rode by, not exactly staring yet taking it all in, the half-dozen shiny vehicles parked at an angle to the road on what had been the front lawn of a newish, single story house with an attached, two-car garage; a garage door— the one on the right open—and in front of it, further to the right and parked on the lawn, the red Corvette I'd seen several times in and around the village. I thought I'd glimpsed motion inside the open garage bay but I could have imagined it.

I thought about Alan Ames as I rode. I wondered what the dynamics of my family were like now that he'd become a part of the household. From things he'd said and his facial expressions, I believed Seth saw through him. Molly, on the other hand...I'd lost track of her age, had her locked in a sort of time warp, stuck at about age twelve, still a kid. It was difficult for me to wrap my head around the fact that she was now an adolescent of fifteen, a young woman with well-defined shape, already using make-up and...Maggie's breathless description of Mr. Ames came to mind. If a worldly-wise and worn widow, mother of six middle-aged "kids" and grandmother to some twenty—she said at last count—could find Mr. Ames that attractive, I could only imagine his effect on an impressionable teenager. How trustworthy was he? Could Ellen control the situation? Given her work schedule, would she even be totally aware of everything that went on at home?

In more ways than one, my ex's household presented an ideal target for any man with nefarious intentions. Aside from my blossoming, impressionable, highly vulnerable teenage daughter, Ellen herself made an alluring target for some man scheming for what would appear to be an easy, carefree life. First, the house was without a doubt among the largest and nicest of private homes in the area. Then, with Harry's condition deteriorating by the day, she faced the certain prospect of inheriting a fair amount of money as well as her parent's house, which was easily worth upward of four-hundred thousand. I doubted she would be entirely reticent about discussing her financial prospects, especially in a social setting in which she wanted to look good.

Ellen had her faults but I'd always given her credit for working hard. Blanche had persuaded her to get her bachelor's degree in management. I remembered my mother-in-law saying once she'd hoped Ellen would go on for a masters, get herself hired at some prestigious company and rise to the top, ultimately becoming a CEO. Failing that, she'd said—and this was exactly how she had phrased it—"You can always come back here and manage Harry's business." I remembered not only the words but her disparaging tone, as though Harry's business was insignificant and also implying that Harry needed help managing it.

Ellen hadn't gone on for her masters, marrying me instead, much to her mother's chagrin. She had, however, taken a very good job at a small, local company which manufactured electronic parts for several major corporations as well as the U.S. military. The company had grown over the years to become the largest in Collinsville and Ellen had worked her way up into a management position. It hadn't been an easy climb because she'd had to compete with equally well qualified men and, of course, had taken a few months of maternity leave after each of the kids was born. I had no idea what her salary had risen to but I did know how much our household expenses were each month—including the high mortgage—and knew that my child support payments represented a modest contribution to her total costs.

As I rode along, I thought about all these advantages an Alan Ames might take stock of in Ellen if he were trolling for an eligible woman and a warm place to crawl into.

On Wednesday morning I bicycled the half-mile to the nursing home, hoping Harry would be awake and perhaps be comforted by a visit. They were still gathering breakfast trays when I arrived and it appeared someone had just finished feeding Harry, leaving remnants of an unappetizing green mush in a bowl on the stand by his bed. His eyes brightened somewhat as I leaned over and spoke. It wasn't much of a response but enough that I made small talk for the next few minutes. I told him about the kids returning to school, said they both sent their love and that I knew they'd rather be there visiting in person to say Hi. I told him there was a good chance Todd would be landing a contract to build a new condo complex on the mountain and that if he did I'd be getting back to work. I mentioned the fine weather, how I'd been biking each day to stay in shape and that Al at the Collinsville Banner was still keeping me employed part-time and staying out of trouble. He seemed to take it all in. But as I looked down to say Good-bye, I saw in his withered face a desperate plead- ing for release.

Rounding a corner in the hallway on my way out, I nearly collided with Julie. She appeared as flustered as I felt. For a split second or two, neither of us could seem to find words.

She broke the awkward silence. "Hi Mark. Ralph's back. He found a job." It came out in a rushed, though restrained monotone; her eyes were downcast.

"Great, Julie! I'm glad to hear it. Full-time?"

"Yes. Another delivery driver job. Snacks, and pastries."

"Very good. He must be thrilled to be driving again, finally pulling down a paycheck."

"Oh, he is," she said in the same flat, unemotional tone and with little facial expression. She paused, appearing on the verge of adding to it and then said simply, "Well, good seeing you, Mark. Got to run."

"Good seeing you, Julie. Take care, now, and please tell Ralph how happy I am for him."

"I will."

I'll be the first to admit that I've never been good at reading the minds of women. Maybe that's a confession most men ought to make if they choose to be objectively, brutally honest. Julie's blank expres- sion and curtness could have reflected regret over our love-making, her feeling of shame for having cheated on Ralph, or then again, if she had truly felt all the negative things she'd said about Ralph, her demeanor could have signaled disappointment that he'd moved back home. In any case, I felt sorry for her. I also knew that if it wasn't in complete tatters, my friendship with both Julie and Ralph would cer- tainly be strained in the future.

Following a quick noontime sandwich and cup of coffee back at my apartment I hit the road biking again, now planning to ride the same eighteen mile route Ralph and I had often taken. The afternoon was warm and sunny— reason enough to justify the hour and a half of outdoor activity—but in an odd way my decision also seemed related to Julie's news about Ralph. Deep down I cared for both Julie and Ralph, as individuals and as a couple. It had distressed me a week earlier when Julie had told me Ralph had left; she'd made the hurt still worse when she had so vehemently put him down. Perhaps this long, enjoyable ride ahead—the same route I'd taken several times with Ralph—was my means for celebrating his reemployment and return to his family.

Ralph probably wasn't as ambitious as he could or should be. He did look overweight and out of shape. Neither a father nor a mother should ever express disappointment in the gender of their kids, either by their actions or in carelessly-guarded words.

There was a flip side, however. I had mentally registered refutations to nearly all of Julie's complaints against Ralph. I'd never been a route delivery driver, never wanted to be one, yet I could imagine how fifteen years at that sort of work could lead to being overweight and out of shape. There is some lifting, some carrying, for sure, but delivery drivers use dollies. Perhaps Ralph had put in long days and hadn't felt like getting regular exercise outside of the job. Over the years I'd seen any number of overweight truck drivers and imagined they might often nibble on food, snacks or candy to assuage the boredom.

I could understand Ralph's frame of mind as well, his seeming lack of ambition. I was unemployed—make that underemployed—myself and knew first hand the emotional pain from losing a job and the aftermath effects, the soul-searching, the loss of self-confidence and self-worth, the powerlessness and desperate feelings of inadequacy. My vocation as a carpenter had formed, and continued to form, a huge part of the bedrock upon which my self-image was built. I knew what it was like having that knocked out from under me. Maybe, unlike Ralph, I'd explored my options more thoroughly. Perhaps my self-esteem hadn't plunged quite as low, which had bolstered my courage sufficiently to approach Al. But the day I had first met Ralph out biking I'd felt that we were kindred spirits, that seeing him was in one sense like looking into a mirror.

As I thought about my current relationship with Molly, I could even to a limited extent understand Ralph's negative feelings about having only daughters. Naturally It would never happen but if a father were to co-parent three children, all daughters and all with Molly's current disposition, he could be forgiven for lamenting not having fathered a son.

I headed on the main route out of town, past the Shell station and on by Mr. Ames' used car establishment. I slowed as before to take in the array of the half-dozen vehicles parked at an angle, mostly sedans with a couple of pickup trucks mixed in. The garage bay on the right was again open and the Corvette was also parked where it had been on Monday. I sped up, trying to put Alan Ames out of my mind.

A couple of miles beyond the used car lot I hung a right onto Verge Road, a lightly-traveled gravel road which circles around to the north, eventually leading back to Collinsville village. I'd pedaled only a few hundred yards when disaster struck...

I heard the vehicle coming first, quickly steered far onto the right, soft shoulder...heard the high rate of speed...glanced at the tiny mirror...distortion there, blurriness, a truck grill?...a split second, then I felt the crushing impact, heard the crumpling of tire and metal frame, the engine roar...My head jerked back, a surge of fear, my limp body hurtling airborne, legs caught, entangled in crushed metal...an instant of sickening apprehension, of foreboding...then blankness.

I don't remember my impact with Mother Earth. Likely fortunate. I do remember a gradual return to consciousness...remember the pointy-sharp pain of grit in both lid-locked eyes...remember commanding my left arm to move, move, move...remember the futile answer in excruciating jabs of pain...remember a dull ache in my left leg...remember ordering my lungs to fill with air, and the agonizing response in knife-like stabs of pain up and down my left side... remember my numbing realization that without enough breath my life could ebbe away, that I might be doomed to suffocate as I lay virtually helpless amid a heap of mangled bike parts by the side of Verge Road.

Time passed, measured in shallow gasps for air, each breath shortened by what felt like piercing shards of glass embedded in my lungs. Fractured ribs, I thought, taking inventory of what hurt the most and where in my body. Had to be several. I'd broken two ribs in a careless fall from a ladder years earlier while working for Todd and remembered that type of pain. Maybe a broken left arm?

I tried to move, if only to sit up, but even slight movement caused jolts of agonizing pain along my left side and shoulder. The dull soreness in my left leg suddenly throbbed as I tried to move it Although mobile, my right arm ached and my fingers kept feeling of liquid, doubtless blood. I cursed the grit in my eyes. Each effort to open even one resulted in sharp, nearly unbearable pain which drove my head to ache as well. Deprived of eyesight, I tried not to imagine the worst.

Emily, her name was, the Good Samaritan who pulled off the road at four-twenty, I later learned, and used her cell phone to call 911. She remained close by until the ambulance arrived: my guardian angel, who comforted me like a mother—or perhaps grandmother—in a soft, lilting voice of indeterminate age, telling me in a dozen soothing ways that I'd be okay. With eyes swollen shut, I never saw Emily or even got her last name but I heard she later called the hospital to inquire about my condition before traveling on. They told me she identified herself only as Emily, a tourist from New York state passing through to Maine, that she had taken Verge Road as a short-cut from one major route to another. If there is a Saint Peter at a Pearly Gate, he needs to register a decisive plus mark on the record of a very special lady from New York named Emily.

I did suffer broken ribs. At least six confirmed by ex-rays and a seventh described as possibly fractured. Fractured ribs are generally not life-threatening unless they puncture internal organs, such as lungs;

preliminary examination indicated none of mine apparently had done that. If not too severe, corneal abrasions generally heal within a few days. After removal of grit from both eyes, mine were expected to do just that. My left eye was more badly scratched than the right and did require a patch for two days.

What I had imagined from the pain could be a fractured arm, turned out to be a dislocated left shoulder, which was forcefully manipulated back into place. My right arm had evidently struck a sharp rock or a low-lying pointed tree limb, inflicting a nasty two by four inch gash, the source of the blood I'd felt. The source of pain in my left leg turned out to be a very bad bruise.

And my face...if I were steeped in vanity or less accepting by nature, the cuts criss-crossing my face like butcher marks on a ham could have proven the most devastating of my injuries! Would they leave permanent scars? I knew better than to ask. They would, especially the worst one which required a great many stitches and two others which were protectively covered with large bandages. I chose to think of my impending scars as adding character to an otherwise nondescript face, perhaps one day becoming a subject of speculation: "Wasn't that the courageous fellow so badly wounded by shrapnel in one of the wars?"

I was admitted to the hospital for that night as a precaution in case the broken ribs had caused internal injuries, then released at mid-afternoon the following day when the doctor was reasonably certain they hadn't. It got complicated, for one thing because I had nothing to wear (my biking shorts and jersey were shredded as well as filthy) and I also would need to call on someone to drive me home. I debated calling Al but phoned Todd instead, arranging for him to swing by the hospital first to pick up my apartment key which, luckily, was still in the fanny pack the ambulance crew had thought to load aboard with me. I took a guess that my cell phone had been lost, but that was the least of my worries. I'd been wearing a helmet, too, but...

Todd's cheery greeting when all of this was accomplished and I was waiting in a wheelchair at the curb? "Damn, Mark, there's better looking than you down at the morgue!"

"No jokes, Todd!" I warned him. "I can't laugh, sneeze, cough—hell, it hurts to breathe."

"Tough break," he said, opening the passenger side door of his pickup.

I was grateful for the stepped running board on his truck. Turning to thank the nurse who had wheeled me out, I said she deserved a tip and would normally get a generous one except that I had no money!

True friends are the people who rally around you when trouble strikes, the ones who know exactly what you'll need and who generously provide it. In my case, it was Todd who stopped by at least once each day over the next four to offer transportation and to simply chat; Maggie who brought delicious casseroles twice and grocery shopped on Monday; Al, who stopped in briefly a couple of times, again offering a few bucks to tide me over, phrasing it in terms of a loan to preserve my pride; and yes, on Saturday morning, even Ralph dropped in to offer sympathy along with his and Julie's best wishes for my quick recovery.

The law caught up with me early on Friday morning, with Chief Clem McDonald knocking on my door at eight-ten, informing me that a State Police Trooper named Sgt. Kevin Waterman would "be right along in a couple of minutes" and handing me my cell phone, then my bike helmet. "I got there right after the ambulance left," he said, "and found the phone lying over near some bushes. Must have flown a good thirty feet out of your pocket. It is yours, right?"

I assured him it was, invited him in for coffee but he said he had to get back to the office. Said he was sorry to hear it was me who'd been struck on a bicycle; also glad he happened to be free to help the State Police by going out and waiting until they could send somebody to take over.

"Of course it's outside the village limits," he said, informatively, "so it's up to them to handle it. Any idea who it might have been?"

I shook my head. "Not a clue. Possibly an SUV or a pickup truck, but it all happened so fast."

He shook his head also. "Half these kids think you can drive without looking at the road," he said, disgustedly. "Used to be drinking and driving, then drugs, and now they're all texting, or whatever." He shook his head again for good measure, then politely asked the extent of my injuries.

I kept it brief, ending by saying I was very, very lucky, that it could have been so much worse. "I know I look like death warmed over, Clem, but I feel considerably better than I look."

"I hope so, Mark."

Sgt. Kevin Waterman got there a few minutes after Clem left. Medium height, stocky, a firm handshake, professional but personable, about my age—maybe the best age for a law officer: over being self-important and inflated with the sense of power that often accompanies the donning of a uniform. Unlike Clem, he entered my humble abode, accepted an offer of coffee, and, with clipboard in hand, sat down on the raggedy sofa. Being called "Mr. Sloan" seemed strange at first but I got used to it.

After the preliminary personal questions and inquiry regarding my injuries, Sgt. Waterman took down my account of what had happened. He'd been on the scene, apparently with another officer, they'd measured, photographed, gotten good clear tire prints in the sandy soil, had confirmed that the vehicle had swung "a good three feet" off the packed road bed where it had struck me, and they had recovered shattered glass from a headlight. "A few other miscellaneous pieces," he added, "which might or might not have been part of the grill or bumper. We have somebody who should be able to analyze those."

He characterized my bike as "history," and probably not even good for parts. "Except," he said, pausing thoughtfully to qualify it, "as evidence. There's a long scratch on the frame. Mostly down to the bare metal but there's a faint streak of black paint there. Not much, but enough to show up against the white. Wouldn't be primer paint, not black under white, so...we're thinking the vehicle could have been black."

As part of the investigation, he said, they'd be paying visits to area auto body shops. "The passenger side front end of whatever struck you has to be fairly well smashed."

He said his department would do all it could to track down and charge the guilty hit-and-run driver, not only to be held accountable for the legal violations in the accident but so that I could collect damages and pay my medical expenses. "I hate to think what your medical bills are going to run, Mr. Sloan."

I gulped, thinking about that very same thing.

Picking up on his phraseology, I gathered Sgt. Waterman was assuming what had happened to me was accidental. He went on, briefly mentioning other tragic incidents in the State.

"I don't know if you've followed the news, Mr. Sloan," he said, "but we've had several biking accidents like this around the State this summer. One fatality in Burlington and another up in Derby. One of those was alcohol and drug related and the other was a girl texting. We had a runner get struck and killed up in Swanton in June. A drunk driver in that case. Oh, and we've had at least three flagger incidents, one of those was fatal. Alcohol is the biggest factor but texting is a growing problem. All of it's worse with speed."

I debated telling him about the other suspicious incidents, about the failed brakes, the peanut oil, my previous close call while biking. I knew that I'd later regret not mentioning the biking near mishap, that at least it had been witnessed by Ralph who would verify what he had seen. I went ahead with that much and he took notes as I related the incident.

"Ralph thought it was a black truck," I concluded, "but like this time, it happened so fast neither one of us got a good look at either the driver or the truck."

"I agree it probably doesn't have a bearing, but I'll include it in the report for the record. Anyway, in this case, even if it was caused by carelessness, alcohol... distracted driver, whatever, you've suffered some serious injuries. The fact is, the driver fled the scene. We'll do the best we can, Mr. Sloan, to find out who it was and go from there. Needless to say, if you remember anything else important or see or hear something that might help us, don't hesitate to give us a call"

As he stood up to leave, Sgt. Waterman gave me his card and at the door wished me a speedy recovery.

# 15

I WOULD HAVE dreaded Ralph's visit Saturday morning if he'd called first to let me know he was dropping by. But he didn't, and the surprise made it easier.

"Read about it in today's Collinsville Record," he said. "I wanted to bring it but Julie went to work early so didn't get a chance to read it. I'll save it for you, though."

"Thanks, Ralph. Yeah, I'd like to read it but don't make a special trip." I hadn't given a thought to the fact that the daily would run a story. I hoped Al would keep it out of the Banner. Some people enjoy publicity but I'm definitely not one of them. Especially regarding a damn biking accident.

Ralph and I had a good conversation. Much as I hoped he wouldn't, he went into detail about leaving Julie and the kids for several days. Said he'd packed his tent and camping gear and gone to a campground to stay and "sort things out." He'd missed them every minute he'd been away, he said, but he and Julie had done nothing but fight over his not finding work and he simply couldn't deal with all the pressure.

"She didn't get it, Mark, she just didn't get it. I know what I can do and what I can't. I don't need anybody nagging. Telling me I'm not trying hard enough, or not ambitious enough. Saying I'm...how'd she put it… 'Wallowing in self-pity.' Yeah, that was it. Wallowing in self-pity. Nobody wants to hear that crap. Do you know what I mean?"

"I do." I did.

"The thing is, yes, I could have gone to work at McDonald's and mopped the floor. Sure. Minimum wage! Big frigin' deal! We'd have been ahead a few bucks maybe. But how the hell would that have made me feel? Having everybody I know coming in and pitying me. Feeling sorry for Julie and the kids and thinking I must be a damned loser! The other thing is, if you're working even part-time it takes you away from looking for the job you really want. No, I had to do it my way, try the best I could to get back into driving, which is what I know. Which I'm good at and pays a hell of a lot more than minimum wage!"

"Ralph, I know what you're saying because I've been there. And sounds like you've succeeded. You did it right and it's obviously paid off. So things are…well…sort of back to normal, are they with, well, Julie and the kids?" I scanned his face for a sign, any indication of how things were going. Confirmation that Julie hadn't told Ralph anything about…

His hesitation was momentary, a split second which I picked up on. "Oh yeah, pretty much. I think Julie's still put out that I left. Maybe pissed that doing it my way panned out better than if I'd taken a part-time scrounge job like she wanted. But, yeah, things are getting back. As far as the girls…probably doesn't make much difference to them."

"More than you know, Ralph, more than you know," I said, heaving a gentle sigh of relief. "Kids don't always express their feelings."

"Well, that's true enough."

I asked him how much the new job was like the old one driving bread truck; heard more detail than I'd anticipated or thoroughly understood, but that was okay. The bottom line was that Ralph was back to full-time delivery driving and liked the job so far. He seemed upbeat and much happier. Maybe most important of all to me, Ralph apparently knew nothing of my one-time, intimate relationship with his wife.

When Todd stopped in later during the afternoon on Saturday, after telling me there was nothing new on the condo project, he kicked off our speculation over who the hit-and-run driver might have been. First, was it accidental or on purpose? I told him Clem and Trooper Waterman both had seemed to assume it was accidental, a drunk, drugged or distracted driver who simply swung too far to the right.

"Waterman went on at great length reciting the statistics," I said, "how many runners, flaggers and bikers have been struck by cars in Vermont this summer. I don't know why he thought it was relevant except maybe to show how dangerous the roads are. The thing I keep coming back to is that according to him, I was a good three feet off the side of the road. As far as I'm concerned it has to be more than a coincidence. I mean to lose control that badly, at that specific spot in the road."

"Yeah, I see your point. And didn't you say you think he speeded up? At the last second you heard the engine race?"

I nodded. "I can't be sure. Can't swear to it, but yeah. It was awfully loud."

Todd had remembered my telling him and Ben about the failed brake and peanut oil incidents. "Did you say anything to Waterman about those?" he asked.

"No, but I did mention almost being hit back a few weeks ago when Ralph Swartz and I were out out biking. I guess I didn't have a chance to tell you about that ..." I said, continuing on to describe what had happened.

"So that was a black truck too?"

"Yeah. I wasn't paying attention but Ralph said it was."

He shook his head slowly. "Boy, I don't know, Mark. A lot of black rigs around. For a while, everybody was buying dark blue but now about every other rig you see is black, the new ones, anyway."

"I know. And it comes down to motive."

Almost simultaneously, we both though of Roger Dornier.

Todd said, "His newest truck does happen to be black, Mark. I don't know if you've seen it."

"No."

"Another Ford, of course. That whole family is into Fords. I think this is a 350, same as his last one."

"Brandy new?"

"Yup. Saw him driving it yesterday. Business must be good for Roger."

"Yeah, a hell of a lot better than for the rest of us." I paused for a moment then went on, "But think about it, Todd. Can you really, I mean really, imagine Roger Dornier smashing into me with his brand new F-350? Doing damage to his fender?"

"Well...no. Not hardly."

"Just out of spite. That and because he's afraid of whatever else I might dredge up and persuade Al to print?"

"Well..." he considered it pensively.

"I don't either. The more I've thought about it, the less likely it seems. I think he's got Al in his pocket anyway. Knows Al won't print anything too damning for fear of losing the advertising. And I'm not being critical of Al here, trust me, because Al grubs out a living like the rest of us. He isn't making a fortune on the paper, in fact I'd say some weeks he's subsidizing it."

Todd looked thoughtful. "So who else might want you out of the way?"

"Good question. I wish I knew."

"Tell you what," he said, "I can at least go by the gun shop on the way home and see if his truck's parked in front."

"Thanks, Todd."

Maggie's three relief missions to my apartment those days I spent licking my wounds were a blessing. On Friday and again Sunday she stopped by briefly to deliver casseroles; on Monday she did a grocery store run, in spite of my telling her I felt able to do it myself. It was that day when she stayed longer, accepted an offer of coffee and sat for a few minutes to chat. It turned out her purpose included more than keeping me stocked in groceries.

"Al would kill me if he knew I was discussing this," she began by way of warning, "so if you breathe a word I'll flat out deny it. Understand?"

"Sure, I guess, but what— "

"I mean it, Mark. Only between us."

"Okay, okay!" Hard to put on a face of persuasive reassurance when your face is half bandaged and laced with stitches.

A final pause in hesitation, and then she said, "Al and I go back a ways, as you've probably gathered. I guess I know him better than, well, most people. Most people only know what he thinks. Hell, you'd have to be deaf or illiterate in this town not to know what Big Al Fortin thinks. But that's only part of Al, the crusty part," she said, her voice growing even deeper, huskier. "There's ton's more under all that bluster, Mark. Under all the toughness and strong opinions, believe it or not, Al's a pretty sensitive guy. Most folks know what Al's thinking but hardly anybody knows what he's feeling. What's going on inside. You understand what I'm saying?"

"I do know what you're saying, Maggie. I've caught glimpses of it." I considered mentioning his repeated offer of money but decided against it. "And you're right," I went on, "Al doesn't wear his feelings on his sleeves. Maybe it goes along with being so big. Having to live up to the image."

"Could be. Partly, anyway. It's also a generational thing. Our generation. Al and I are about the same age. We were taught to hold our emotions in, you know. Things you simply didn't discuss, even with people close to you. Like secrets, you keep them to yourself. How you felt wasn't considered important so you were discouraged from talking about it. Nobody wanted to hear it, for one thing."

"I've gotten that impression from my parents," I said, nodding.

"Sure. It's true. Anyway, Al hasn't shared a lot of what he's feeling but enough that I know the paper isn't as important to him now as it was in the past. Especially when he first took it over. It's...how can I put it...I think it's becoming more of a burden than something he's excited about. He won't admit it, even to me, but I can tell. I don't mean it's dragging him down, but the joy's isn't there any more. I think he sees himself in a...well, in a rat race. He isn't having fun anymore. He used to enjoy plunging into all the local issues. Get all fired up, lock horns with this one and that one, blast away and get a real kick out of doing it. For the last year though, his heart hasn't been in the fight. Not that the issues aren't still worth fighting over, they are. It's just that he's being pulled in too many directions. Having to please one idiot over here," she said, motioning with her hand to the left, "and then kowtow to this jerk over here...it isn't Al's style, you know? Being forced into doing it isn't Al's way. I'm afraid it's starting to take a toll on him."

I remembered the term which had come to mind several times earlier and tried it out: "Compromise. You're saying Al's having to compromise his principles. That's it, isn't it?"

"Exactly!" she said, pouncing on it. "Having to compromise his principles is tearing him apart inside. He says he's never in his life had to work at a job in which he couldn't be himself. Couldn't call a spade a spade. Tell somebody where to shove it if he had to. And now he's having to be more careful what he says and writes. Has to make sure he doesn't step on people's toes. Running the paper used to be fun but now he I think he's feeling it's nothing more than a job."

"One in which he's having to say and write things he doesn't always believe."

"Exactly. And something else that came up when we were talking the the other day. He was saying how creating, well, really building, is quite different from maintaining. The skill sets, as he put it, are different. He said it took his particular skill set to save the Banner from going under. He said it was more like a hobby when he started out. A challenge to take something that was headed down and to build it back up. But now the Banner needs maintaining. He says the skill set for maintaining is entirely different. That's part of the problem, too—he's bored."

"It's an interesting distinction, isn't it. And I can see it." I could see it because I'd thought that same matter through weeks earlier when I'd agonized over what type of work to look for after being laid off from the work I loved. What I couldn't see was where Maggie was going with it. "So what does Al want to do?" I asked. On a hunch I added, "Or what do you think he should do?"

Easy to tell when an emotional cord was struck in Maggie. Her well-lined face would instantly flush. "Well, that's what I'm getting at, Mark. When I said just now that Al doesn't always let on how he feels, I meant including how he feels about you and your work."

"Me?"

"Yes, you. Al will never say it himself. Not to your face I mean. But he thinks the world of you, Mark. I don't want to embarrass you, but Al has nothing but praise for you and the work you've been doing as a reporter. I've lost count of the number of times he's told me you have the right stuff, as he puts it, the right stuff as a reporter and even as an editor."

"Well, I—"

"No, it's true. He doesn't have to change a thing in any of the stories you write. I can't tell you how much he's raved over your coverage of the wind project, for instance. Your understanding of all the complicated facets of it and then how well you've explained it in laymen's terms which make sense to people. You probably had no idea how much he appreciated your features on the nursing home, either, but he praised you sky-high to me. Told me once you're like a bloodhound going after the facts. Digging in, not giving up. "

She paused for a second, then, "I'm sorry...by the look on your face I can see I'm embarrassing you," she said, grinning, "But it's all true, I swear."

She'd nailed it regarding my embarrassment. I felt flattered for sure. Remembering my conversation with Al only a few days earlier, however, and my resolve to stop putting myself down, I didn't refute what she'd said but simply thanked her for her kindness in relaying Al's compliments. I told her what I thought of Al, that I'd grown more and more fond of him as time went on. Then I had to confess I hadn't sensed any boredom on his part with the paper. "Just the other day," I pointed out, "he was mentioning his ad sales in New Hampshire and that circulation is up."

"Oh yes. He's still into the business side, but less into the news. He's discouraged over a lot of the changes, the wind project, for instance. Thinks a lot of locals aren't being heard, that too many people have conflicts of interest. He used to believe he could have an influence with the Banner. Have a say and people would listen. He says there's less civility out there now than when he bought the paper. I think the bottom line, Mark, is that he's tired. He's almost at the point old Mac McDougall was at when he sold Al the paper."

I swallowed hard, then said, "I had no idea, Maggie. I hope you're wrong."

"Oh, I don't mean he's planning on selling any time soon. It's just that, well, Al hasn't come right out and said it," she continued, "not in so many words, but he's broadly hinted that you'd be the ideal person to take over the Banner."

"What!" I'd said it so forcefully a chorus of sharp pains resonated from my ribs.

"I'm only throwing it out there, Mark. As I've said, Al would probably be furious with me for getting into it with you. It isn't so far fetched, though, is it?"

"Except that you've listed a dozen reasons why Al should give it up. He's having to compromise his integrity, he's bored, he's sick and tired of kowtowing to the idiots and jerks...Maggie, why on earth... "

"Because you're younger, for one thing. Al's sixty-nine. He's tired, sick of the rat-race. But for somebody younger like you it would be a challenge, just as it was for Al when he bought the paper."

My thoughts were so scrambled I didn't know where to begin. Without the luxury of time to prioritize, I said, "You're forgetting I'm flat broke. I've been surviving pay check to pay check combined with unemployment benefits. I'm barely able to pay the rent here, the child support, keep my truck on the road—Maggie, the last thing I can consider is buying Al out!"

She looked prepared. "I'm sure it would surprise you, but I have a strong suspicion that for you, Al would turn over the Banner for very little money. In fact, I think he'd practically give it to you. Either outright or his terms would be so generous you couldn't refuse the offer."

I stayed focused on money. "That would be wonderful and unbelievably generous of Al," I said, "and of course I'd feel grateful. The thing is, Maggie, I've watched Al struggle, trying to make ends meet with the Banner. I know he says it's a money-maker now, that ad sales are up. But I've suspected right along that Al's been subsidizing it. I figured from his Social Security."

She looked taken aback. Then what I'd read as shock on her face turned to one of the broadest grins I'd ever seen Maggie wear. (Well, except for the day she interviewed Alan Ames.) "Oh, my poor dear boy!" she laughed. "Hon, you've been royally bamboozled! Al Fortin doesn't subsidize the paper. Trust me on that. I keep his books." She paused for a couple of seconds, then went on, "You'd have no way of knowing, Mark, but Al and I are...shall we say closer than you might have guessed. Yes, I do his books. I don't know a lot about his finances but I can assure you Al is very well off financially. Naturally you wouldn't know it by listening to him. Or the way he dresses or the clunker he drives. But I'd compare Al to one of those bag ladies you sometimes read about. They plead poverty and live like paupers. Nobody suspects the kind of money they have stashed away. Incidentally, that isn't to go beyond these walls, not a word of it," she warned. "And as far as the Banner is concerned, hell, it's made money for him since day one. Since he took over."

Stunned, I must have sat with my mouth gapping open.

"Surprised, huh?" she asked.

"Yeah, that's an understatement," I said.

"Well, Al is full of surprises, believe me."

"So...so," I tried gathering my thoughts, managing to come up with something pitifully weak and rhetorical: "What would he do? I mean if he sold the paper?"

She looked away momentarily, then back. "Al? Again, hon, this is between you and me and the gatepost, but even old folks like us can dream. I'm not exactly down to my last pair of shoes either, if you know what I mean. So before you go jumping to any conclusions— "

"Which I obviously have a piss-poor track record doing," I interjected.

"Yes, so far you do, hon," she acknowledged with a knowing nod. "Put it this way. Al hasn't thrown away any of the Viking Cruise brochures I've left lying around. And last Friday I noticed he'd circled a couple of the homes in a Florida real-estate magazine I'd left on his desk."

Sleep proved elusive Monday night. My ribs ached, my cut-up face ached, my shoulder ached, I had stubbornly skimped on taking the pain meds the doctor had prescribed; thrown into the mix was the curious conversation I'd had with Maggie, the mental rehashing of which mingled with the pain to keep me awake.

Although I didn't doubt for a minute anything she'd said about Al having money or the Banner making money, I'd found it disconcerting to learn how wrong I'd been on both counts. Then there was the meat of her message, wanting me to consider buying the newspaper. I felt flattered, no way around it. I'd known Al was happy with my work and I'd detected editorial changes to only two of my stories. Being happy with my work however, was a far cry from thinking of me as his ideal successor in owning the paper.

As crazy as the idea of buying the Banner had seemed while Maggie and I had talked, a part of me counseled giving it more consideration.

Was it really that crazy? I understood most of what Al did each week in putting the paper together. Not the mechanics, maybe, of actually laying the pages out and getting them ready for the printer's, but how difficult could learning that process be? I'd always taken pride in being able to learn new things quickly, provided they were logical.

Maggie had laid to rest my mistaken notion the Banner wasn't profitable. If Al could turn a profit, if he'd done it from the beginning, why couldn't I do the same? Didn't I like the idea of being independent? Wasn't I currently unemployed, my only prospect resting on the uncertainty of Todd's winning in the stiff competition for a contract to build a limited number of condominiums? And if Al had that much faith in my ability shouldn't I have as much faith in myself?

Then again...the objections I'd raised with Maggie were equally valid. If she was right, if owning and operating the Collinsville Banner was driving Al over the edge, why on earth would I want to take it on and possibly suffer the same fate? Would I be willing to compromise my integrity, to self-censor in order to retain the likes of a Roger Dornier as a lucrative advertiser? To remain silent on some issue I felt strongly about only to stay in the good graces of certain people in town or a majority of people, many of whom might cancel their subscriptions?

The builder versus maintainer issue we'd discussed was also interesting. I'd been over that same ground in the past and hadn't reached a satisfying answer as to which I was. On the one hand, I loved carpentry. Building. But on the other, I had never had any aspiration to leave Todd and begin a contracting business of my own. Building was creating, in a sense very similar to news and feature story writing. If I'd never toyed with the idea of becoming a building contractor why would I consider owning a weekly newspaper? All of these vexing questions swirled in my head, commingling with my aches and pains into the wee hours of the morning.

# 16

I APPRECIATED VERY much Seth's phone call on Tuesday, the second time he had checked in with me since the accident. The first one he'd made Saturday evening after his mother had read about me in the Collinsville Record. His concern over me in the first call was genuine enough; I hadn't doubted for a minute that calling me was his idea, not his mother's. His call late Tuesday afternoon, however, struck me as odd. The concern in his voice was as real as on Saturday but soon into the conversation I learned that calling me this time had actually been suggested by someone else: Alan.

"I told him you said before you were okay, dad," Seth said. "But he wanted me to check and make sure again."

"Well, that was very thoughtful of Alan," I said. "Very thoughtful. So…I take it he's there?"

"Yeah, he got home early. Molly's here too."

"Your mom isn't home from work yet?"

"No. Not yet. Oh, wait…" his voice trailed off as though he had turned from the phone. After a minute he came back on, saying, "I think she's here now, dad. I heard a car in the driveway."

"Oh, probably. Anyway, so Alan thought you should call?"

"Yeah, even though you said it before."

"Huh. Well, be sure to thank Alan for me. No I'm doing fine, buddy. Gaining every day. The shoulder is still a little sore and the ribs still hurt but that's normal. The doctor said it could be a few weeks before the ribs stop hurting, especially when I laugh or cough. I'm still hobbling a little on my left leg because of the bruise and my face is a mess and will be until the cuts heal. But I'm on the mend. In fact I drove today, first time since the accident. Oh, and did I mention on Saturday that the bike is junk?"

"No. Really?"

"Yeah. Totally smashed, I guess. I haven't seen it but that's what they told me."

"Bummer."

"Yeah. At least it wasn't new, but I liked it all the same. I'll have to pick up another one if I can. Probably a good used one." No probably about it. Absolutely a used one. Given the prices, I certainly couldn't afford to buy a new bike.

We talked for a minute about how school was going, how he liked his new teachers, and then I mentioned the upcoming weekend, my turn to have the kids—or more likely Seth alone. "What would you like to do?" I asked.

"I don't know, dad. What can you do?"

Perceptive, I thought. What could I do, with broken ribs and a face which looked and felt like it had suffered a confrontation with a meat grinder? "One thing we really should do is visit Grandpa Harry. Maybe we'll do that early on Saturday."

"Sure, dad, let's. And than if it's a nice day, maybe swimming?"

"Sounds good," I said, chuckling, "but don't expect me to swim with you."

"No, I won't...oh it's mom. I think she's coming in now..." Again a long pause and then his voice as though from a distance: "It's dad." A pause, and back to me, "She says she wants to talk to you. She's coming. Bye, dad."

As I waited I still wondered why Ellen's pretty-faced boy-toy cared about my health. It didn't make sense. I did see a bit of humor in my circumstances, though. I mean, a guy could get a swelled head hearing that his boss thinks he's qualified to take over the business and then learning that his ex-wife's lover is hungry for news of his health! I also wondered why she wanted to talk. I'd scraped up enough money to pay the child support for the month. Hadn't shorted her there. Was it to extend her sympathy? Inquire regarding my injuries?

She picked up and said, "If you're calling about the weekend, Mark, Seth can go but Molly can't. Just thought I should make it clear right now." No preliminaries. No How are you feeling? Not even a Hi Mark.

"Seth called me," I said, "and I know better than to ask if Molly wants to join us. It's been close to a month now that I haven't seen or heard from Molly. Well, except briefly over the phone on Saturday. You said she can't come over...you mean she doesn't want to. Which is fine."

"No, I meant what I said. She can't. Her therapist said it would be best if she didn't see you for awhile."

"Therapist? What therapist?"

"Hers."

"I didn't know anything about a therapist. How long has she been seeing a therapist?"

"Oh, for about two months," she paused for a second, then said, "No, longer than that. I took her before school ended in June. The school counselor recommended she get professional help."

"I didn't know anything about it," I said, easing down onto my decrepit couch in partial shock.

"There are a lot of things you don't know about, Mark. Or don't care about, especially when it comes to Molly. Anyway, Nora said—she's her therapist—said your relationship is so toxic right now it would be best if Molly doesn't have to be with you at all for awhile. I see where she's coming from and I agree."

The word Toxic struck at me like a fist punch to the gut. "Toxic?" I said, recoiling. "This mental health therapist is calling me toxic?" Toxic: a word used to describe medical or nuclear waste. Polluted air. Deadly chemicals. Toxic?

"Not you personally. But your relationship with Molly. Don't sound so surprised. What would you call it?"

"Dysfunctional, maybe, but...toxic?"

"That's just a semantic difference, Mark. The fact remains, you don't have a healthy relationship with her. The only way she's going to get better is if she has as little to do with you as possible. At least until she shows improvement and can deal with it."

"Why didn't you tell me all this before?"

"Because I didn't think you'd particularly care. Mark, you've never—"

"Didn't care? That isn't true Ellen and you know it!"

"Stop hollering. I can hear you. I just came through the door from work and I'm tired. The last fringing thing I need is a bunch of hassling from you!"

"So what the hell's wrong with her? What's the problem?"

"Okay. Nora says it's mainly anxiety but also depression. She doesn't think she's suicidal except there's been some cutting. On her arms and legs. Maybe her ribs too. But not her wrists. Not yet. She was bleeding in class one day before school ended and the teacher sent her to the nurse. That's when they found out. About the cutting, I mean. That's when the nurse called me."

"I don't know what you mean by cutting. Did somebody cut her? Like with a knife?"

I heard her make a "tisk" sound and then sigh deeply before going on. "Mark, you don't have a clue, do you. It's what teenagers are doing today, especially the girls. It's how they're coping. One of the only ways they can cope with anxiety. They're cutting themselves. It relieves the stress they're feeling. The emotional stresses that teenagers are under today."

"That's sick! So what's Molly stressed about?"

"My god, If you don't know, what can I say! You're living in a bubble, I guess. There's a million stresses out there. All the violence in the world, to begin with. School shootings, terror threats, global warming, not to mention the recession and wars. There's a constant stream of—"

"Okay, okay, I get that, but what's it got to do Molly?"

"Mark, these kids are all connected, in case you haven't noticed. She's on line all day and night. Instagram. Twitter and Facebook. She's always in contact with her friends. With everybody at school. Have you even heard of bullying?"

"Of course I've heard of it. What the hell…" I couldn't think straight.

"So it's a serious problem. They're trying to cut down on bullying at school but it's still going on. Everything the kids write about themselves and each other is out there. Every comment gets exaggerated. They see it as a big deal. Especially the girls. They take it personally."

"So all they have to do is turn the damned things off!"

"Like I said, Mark. You live in a bubble. You can't just take these things away. For some kids, what they're doing online is more real than…well, reality. Nora thinks it may be that way for Molly. She sees signs of—"

"More real than reality? What's that supposed to mean? My god, Ellen, that makes no sense!"

"Don't holler! My head's starting to ache and I've got to start dinner. But that's where it stands. You're not going to be spending time with Molly for awhile until she's better. I imagine it'll be a relief for you. I mean, you've never really wanted to spend time with her anyway."

Always a final dig, a zinger left until the end before hanging up or leaving the room. I bit hard: "How the hell can you say that, Ellen? You know it isn't true. I love both kids."

"Yeah, yeah. So much that practically every night for years you weren't there to tuck them into bed. To read stories, or even talk to them much after you came home from work. I was the one who did those things. It's all catching up with you, Mark. You can't blame me and you certainly can't blame Molly. Nobody's to blame but you. You brought it on yourself. You're the one who..."

I could hardly contain my anger. I fought off the urge to fling the cell phone across the room. I'd heard it all before. Ad nauseam. Suddenly, every ache and pain in my body flared up; each facial laceration, shoulder and rib bruise now burning and throbbing, each according to its torturing specialty—every conceivable source of pain all the way down my left leg chimed in to contribute to my misery. She was in mid sentence when I clicked the phone off.

Guilty as charged? As with nearly every such issue, the devil lay in the details. Unfortunately, I didn't spend much time with either of the kids during those years I worked at restoring our house. No one could have regretted that fact more than I did. Yes, I'd missed out on the bedtimes, the story-reading. I'd worked late into most nights, digging dirt by hand to create a basement and, when the foundation was completed, tearing out plaster and lathe partitions and walls, building new ones, wiring, insulating, sheet rocking —doing everything required to make the old place livable.

Sure, Ellen was factually correct. But she'd always failed to acknowledge her part, never conceding that the old Hudson place was way more than we should have taken on. Never admitting that a modest house like Ralph and Julie's was way more practical and within our means. Her usual comeback, that we ought to have contracted all the work I'd done, always led to an argument over indebtedness. I had repeatedly pointed out that hiring contractors to do all of the work I'd done would likely have doubled the amount of the mortgage.

Ellen couldn't see it that way. Far from viewing it as a worrisome burden, an embarrassing result of unrestrained indulgence in spending, she seemed to take pride, not only in our fine home but in the fact that we had a higher mortgage than most of the people we knew just starting out. Naturally, I viewed this linking of indebtedness with social status as an abomination of backward logic.

I sat motionless on the couch for perhaps half an hour. Sat staring at a bare wall, mentally fitting Molly into a slot near the top of my list of concerns. Naturally I'd known there was a problem—hard not to have known, going back to at least late spring—but I'd chalked it up to typical teenager angst. I'd felt that as Seth and I were continuing to relate well and because the two kids squabbled much of the time, Molly might have resented my closeness with her brother. I was also the parent who'd more commonly over the years said No to Molly's requests to buy the latest fad items, those must-have things advertised on TV or which "everybody at school" had or was wearing. Ellen would generally cave.

What I'd just heard came as a total shock. From every angle. The business about Molly "cutting" was especially alarming. I couldn't remember ever hearing of the practice but if I had I must have dismissed it as a rare and extreme act of masochism. A sick-minded perversion. Here I sat, cut up and bruised from an accident, my face still bandaged, hearing that my daughter was self-mutilating and had been for months, a symptom of her emotional suffering. Inflicting on herself a physical pain I didn't need to imagine.

Added to that was the fact that Ellen hadn't picked up the phone and told me the very day she'd learned of Molly's problem. Not merely out of courtesy, but as a matter of duty, perhaps even as a legal obligation respecting my rights as a parent, a child support-paying parent at that. Ellen's saying she withheld it from me believing I wouldn't care—that hurt deeply.

Knowing about it now, however, gained me little. My hands were tied. The counselor might be correct that our relationship was so... toxic?...that Molly should be kept away from me. It simplified my life in one way but it certainly didn't help my self-image as a successful parent.

# 17

I STOPPED IN to see Al on Wednesday, mainly to visit, although I also needed to get back to work. He said it was a light week with only one village meeting scheduled, a Zoning Board meeting, which he'd already spoken to Maggie about covering. "I have an idea for a feature story," he added, "but it can wait until you're feeling better."

"I'm feeling fine," I said to him, " even though the bandages and my hobbling probably suggest otherwise."

"Why don't you take it easy this week, Mark. There's nothing all that pressing to do around here. I know it's hard for you to sit still but..."

"It sure is."

"And if you're short of money, why don't you let me give you a—"

"Thanks, Al, but I'm getting by. Really, I appreciate it, but no."

He gave me a Have it your way look. "Incidentally," he said, "we didn't get into it the other day but I assume you haven't heard any-thing from the police? Whether they have any leads on the driver yet?"

I shook my head. "No, nothing. I did tell the trooper about the other time I was almost hit but I don't think he wanted to hear it. He said he'd include it in his report. He gave me the impression almosts don't count." I paused, then remembered to mention another reason for dropping in. "Oh, Al, I hope you aren't including anything about my accident in the Banner this week."

"Of course it's in there. All the news that's fit to print." He cocked his head to one side. "Hey that's a pretty good phrase I just coined. Maybe I'll use it on the front page. Incorporate it into the masthead."

When I left the office minutes later, on a spur of the moment impulse, I pointed the truck in the opposite direction of my apartment, pointed it toward Route Two with a vague intent of returning to the site of the accident on Verge Road. Morbid curiosity, perhaps, or maybe in the recesses of my mind I held out hope that going back might stir some additional memory of the incident. I seemed to recall having once heard of that happening.

The Shell station came and went and just beyond it Alan Ames' used car establishment. I glanced in that direction, took in the row of vehicles parked at an angle, the driveway, the two bay garage—both doors were closed today—and the red Corvette. I drove along the next two miles and hung a right at the familiar turn onto Verge Road. I slowed down approaching the spot, pulled over and parked. I got out and walked over to where I'd landed off the shoulder, saw the graveled and partially grassed area where I'd slammed my head into it, saw where the tall grass was still bent flat, and saw a small limb, possibly the one which had scratched my eyes. I turned and walked along in the direction I had ridden a week earlier, trying to imagine how it had been, to remember something different or additional. I strained to cast my mind back. It proved futile, however. Everything had happened so quickly, the mirror was so small. Discouraged, I got back into the truck.

I was about to continue on, circle toward Collinsville the long way, when it suddenly occurred to me that something was different, not here at the accident site but back on Route Two. At Alan Ames' used car lot. I drove ahead a hundred yards or so, turned around at a pull-off and headed back toward Route Two.

Reaching the car lot I slowed and drove by at a crawl. The garage looked different, of course, because a week earlier the door of the right bay had been wide open and today both doors were closed. Something else was different, however. I'd gotten nearly past when it suddenly occurred to me the line of vehicles looked shorter. I counted them quickly before having to speed up with traffic approaching from behind. There were four sedans and one dark blue, light-duty pickup truck. On the drive back into town I racked my brain for confirmation of the number of pickups I'd remembered seeing the previous Wednesday; there had been two, I would almost have staked my life on it. Two pickup trucks and four sedans in the line-up of used vehicles when I'd bicycled past the Wednesday before.

That evening I called Todd. Preliminaries out of the way—yes, I was sore but gaining each day, and no, he hadn't received a response yet to his condo bid—I asked him if he'd happened to notice the vehicles in Alan Ames used car lot, specifically the number of pickup trucks he'd recently had for sale.

"No," he said, "I haven't gone out Route Two much, probably only once or twice in the last week. But if you wait just a minute, Mark, I'll get our resident expert before he splits for Tom Catting."

Ben came on the line seconds later, first asking me how fast my wheelchair could go, and then whether any of my nurses at the hospital were "hot."

When we'd finally gotten around to seriousness I said, "Odd question, I know, Ben, but I'm wondering if you've noticed what Alan Ames' used car lot on Route Two has had for trucks recently, say within the last week?"

"Why, your's finally had the radish?"

"Not quite. Won't be long though. No, but I'd swear he had two pickups out there a week ago."

"Yup. A blue Toyota Tacoma and a black F-150. Why?"

"Just curious. Guess he must of sold one in the past week. There's only one, the Toyota, on the lot today."

"Huh. Wonder who he suckered into buying that. If I was working I'd consider the Tacoma but that Ford's nothing but a piece of shit."

"Yeah, I don't doubt it. Tacoma's the only one worth buying, I agree."

"What's yours up to."

"Mileage? Oh, I think it just turned 280."

"Jeeeez."

"Yeah, it doesn't owe me anything. Well, Ben, I thank you very much for the information."

"No problem. If the old man ever gets his shit together we'll be back in business. I can hardly wait."

"Neither can I. He's trying, Ben, he's trying. Thanks again and take it easy. Oh," I said quickly, "Is he still right there handy? Your dad?"

"Sure, just a sec."

I debated how to approach it. A delicate matter when one of your kids...

"Hey, Todd, sorry to bother you again but, well, I need to run this thing by somebody else."

"Sure, what's up?"

"It's about Molly, my daughter. You still have...Brian, is it? In high school?"

"Yeah. Sophomore this year. Why?"

"Well, Ellen told me some bad news on the phone last night. Ever hear your boys mention cutting? Something teenagers do to their arms and legs?"

"Cutting? No, the boys haven't but..." he paused, then continued, "Betty mentioned it back last, well, must have been late last spring. She went to some kind of a thing one night at the high school. They had a speaker who talked about teenage problems. Mostly, I think, it was about drugs and suicide. She's right here if—"

"No, that's okay. Just wondering. Guess I'm not up with the times."

"So she's doing it?"

"Molly? Yeah. According to Ellen. I have to find these things out either by accident or when she gets good and ready to tell me. Then it's usually to beat me over the head with. It seems Molly's been in counseling since spring, too. I had no idea."

"Beginning of the summer, I remember you mentioned having trouble with her."

"Yeah. Started about then. Well, just wondering. I'll let you go, Todd. Thanks."

"Oh, I'd forgotten her name," Todd said, just before I clicked off the phone. "Molly? Your daughter?"

"Yeah, Molly."

"Huh," he said, "I wonder if she's the Molly Brian mentions all the time."

"Could be. She's a freshman this year. Looks and acts older. Unfortunately."

"Brian's new at the game. Won't take him long catching up, though. Not with horny brother still in and out of the house."

Later, around eight, I got a call from Harry's sister, Dottie. She wondered if I'd happened to look in on Harry in the past few days. I told her I hadn't been able to, explained why and that I hadn't left my apartment until the day before.

"I'm sorry to hear that, Mark, really sorry," she said. "You've had a rough enough time this summer as it is without that."

I told her I was mending, also lucky in that I was still "between jobs."

"The reason I'm calling," she continued, "is that they called me this afternoon from the nursing home and said Harry's gone down hill to the point that it could be any time now. I take it he's fairly alert but it's mainly his kidney functioning that's failing. They said he could go on for several days but more likely will pass sometime in the next two. Anyway, I've got a gal to cover through Saturday here, so I'm heading out first thing in the morning. Should get over there around nine. I just thought you'd like to know."

"Of course, and I'll meet you there. What about Ellen? Should I..." not something I desperately wanted to volunteer for.

"I just got off the phone with her. I won't bore you with the details but depending upon what we find, she wants us to call her from there."

"Par for the course, isn't it. Some things never change, do they."

We arrived at the nursing home only moments apart on Thursday morning. Dottie apologized when we met in the common area, said she had no idea the extent of my injuries or she wouldn't have called.

I assured her I looked worse than I felt. That except for the ribs, which would take longer to heal, I was feeling much better.

Before going into Harry's room we spoke briefly with the charge nurse who said that although we might not notice any big change in his appearance, Harry's condition had worsened over the last two days, most notably, she said, his renal functioning. "I can't tell you exactly when" she said, "but it'll be soon, which is why I thought we should give you a call."

Dottie thanked her and we went up the hallway and into his room. Harry was asleep when Dottie approached the bed. I held back a few feet, letting her decide whether to wake him up. She leaned over and spoke several words softly. After a minute or two I could see his eyelids open. She spoke again and it looked as though Harry was responding with an ever so faint smile. I waited another minute or two and then, on a glance—an unspoken signal from Dottie—stepped toward the bed. I was soon to regret doing that.

Harry shifted his gaze toward me and within seconds his demeanor darkened, his eyes opened wider and the faint smile gave way to a troubled frown. He grew restless, shaking his head from side to side.

I quickly whispered to Dottie: "I'll wait outside."

"No. Better stay and reassure him," she whispered back. "I'm sure it's the bandages on your face."

I leaned closer, smiled and said, "Hi Harry. It's just me, Mark. Had a little biking accident, that's all. Take more than this to get me down, though. Scratched is all. Really, I'm fine. Just look awful. Seth would be here but he's in school, Harry, so..."

Harry's restlessness had increased. His head shook, his eyes widened as though in fear, his mouth opened and closed as he struggled to speak.

"I'll go," I whispered to Dottie. "I'll wait for you in the lounge area." She agreed it would be best.

When Dottie rejoined me in a quiet corner of the large common room about twenty minutes later she said she had finally requested that Harry be given a mild sedative to calm him down.

My turn to apologize. I said, "I'm sorry, Dottie, didn't give it a thought how bad I look. All the same, I wouldn't have expected that much of a reaction. Would you?"

"No. I agree it was odd. But I certainly don't blame you. You did the right thing by coming. I really appreciate that you did. Before the pill took hold he kept trying to say something. Kept mouthing words but nothing would come out, no sound at all. No air capacity left. I think they're right. I doubt he'll hold on much longer. "

I shook my head slowly in sad agreement. A moment of silence then as I'm sure her thoughts ran similar to mine, that a beloved brother and cherished family member was rapidly slipping away from life.

Before leaving, I said, "I wonder what he was trying to say?"

Dottie shrugged noncommittally. "I do have one idea," she said, "but it's only a guess and it'll have to wait until I know something else for sure. About how he's arranged things." I must have frowned because she added, "I'm sorry to be so vague, Mark, but I'll have to leave at that for now. I could be wrong, too. We may never know what's going through his mind."

Dottie said she planned to stay for a few hours, into the afternoon at least, but had to get back to the dog shelter that night. I offered her any help I could give—meaning it—but got the polite refusal I expected. Dottie was likely a practicing women's libber before Phyllis Schlafly even coined the phrase.

Our parting comments pertained to Ellen. Dottie said, "I'm debating what I'll say to her. Even whether to call yet. As the nurse said, it could be in the next two minutes or the next two days." She looked at me, not really appealing for advice it seemed, but for concurrence on what she'd already decided.

"I guess if it were up to me I'd call and tell her just what the nurse said to us. Two minutes or two days. Let her sort it out with her conscience and busy schedule."

Uncharacteristic, I thought, of Dottie: she winked.

Our nursing home visit on Thursday morning was the last one Dottie and I would make because Harry died in his sleep sometime during that night. I got a call from her mid-morning on Friday. In an unemotional, straight-forward delivery she told me arrangements were in place, that Harry's body would be cremated, that following his wishes there would be neither a church service nor any sort of family or public memorial observance. "As you know," she said, "he wasn't at all religious. One of the finest men I've ever known, and I'm not saying that just because he was my brother, but Harry had has own way of thinking about life and death. It didn't require his having to believe in religion."

It took me a moment to collect myself and yes, to continue speaking with Dottie through welling tears. My throat suddenly swelled at the memory of his agitation at seeing me. "I shouldn't have...gone," I managed in a hoarse voice. "It's my fault he got upset. I shouldn't have—"

"No, Mark," she cut in, "It isn't your fault. Harry wanted to pass and it was time. You did the right thing by being there. It all worked out for the best. Believe me on that."

Dottie's controlled, unemotional tone of voice over the phone proved the perfect antidote to my self-flagellation. In that moment I recalled the previous visit to Harry, when I'd looked down and read a desperate unhappiness in his withered face, a helpless pleading for release. I could accept his passing as a blessing, purely and simply that, which was what Dottie was saying. As I processed it all, I nearly missed hearing what she said toward the end, something about "settling the estate as soon as possible" and that it shouldn't need to go through probate court, that "Harry had paid a good lawyer at Hardy and Danforth to avoid all of that."

I didn't think to ask Dottie if she had contacted Ellen the day or evening before. In a way it wasn't any of my business to ask, nor did it matter. I'd never thought of Ellen as being a bad person, merely a self-centered one with screwed-up values. Probably deep down she loved her father. Maybe she hadn't fully dealt with his having a stroke, or couldn't stand the emotional stress of seeing him decline in a nursing home. Whatever.

# 18

IT RAINED OFF and on Friday so I spent most of the day in my apartment. Not a good thing because the combination of dreary weather, Dottie's sad news and my continuing body aches discouraged a positive attitude. In spite of efforts to look at the bright side— to imagine Todd getting the contract to build the condominiums, to play out a scenario in which I actually bought the Collinsville Banner from Al—my thoughts repeatedly veered toward the negative.

For the first time ever, I even felt apprehensive over picking Seth up on Saturday. How would he accept his grandfather's death? I thought we'd handled the issue as well as possible that last time while fishing at Tyler Pond but that was before Harry had actually died. I wouldn't be taking him to visit Harry tomorrow as we'd planned and as there was to be no funeral or memorial gathering for Harry, neither of the kids would get to experience that traditional custom said to foster closure. The kids' only way of memorializing Harry would be through cherishing their memories of him and that, I thought, was a great shame.

There was another issue churning in my brain on Friday. It concerned my "accident" and connections I was gradually making between it and Alan Ames. I still pondered over why Mr. Ames had urged Seth to call me after school on Tuesday. That seemed more than odd. Added to it was the fact that one of the trucks had disap-peared from his used car lot. Mere coincidence? Of course he could have sold the F-150. He was in business to sell used vehicles. That was the most likely explanation. All the same...maybe at a gut level, the real reason Mr. Ames first came to mind in connection with my bike crash was that over the summer I'd formed an increasingly unfavor-able impression of him. I hadn't yet met him but I knew that I didn't care for Alan Ames.

Looking at it as objectively as I could, I considered the fact that both times, the first when I was nearly struck riding my bike with Ralph and the second last week, had happened only minutes after riding past Mr. Ames' used vehicle lot. A coincidence? The closed door on the right bay of the garage, the bay in which he presumably did repairs and auto-body work—was that another coincidence? His car was parked in front. Could he have been doing body work on the front fender of the missing F-150 pickup?

I thought back to a previous incident, back to the brakes. Setting my truck up for brake failure earlier in the summer would have been child's play for an Alan Ames. I couldn't remember exactly when Molly had first mentioned Alan but time-wise it could have jibed. No way of knowing when Ellen had started dating him. And the peanut oil inci-dent? I suddenly realized that of course, Alan Ames might have had access to my apartment key, depending upon where Seth kept the duplicate I'd given him.

The biggest problem in all of this and what rendered it highly improbable—a figment of my overactive imagination, perhaps—was the fact that Alan Ames had no motive. I came back to that simple fact again and again. There was nothing in it for him, no advantage to accrue from my death. And looked at from Ellen's perspective, until both kids were eighteen I would be a continuing source of monthly income. In the end I had to admit to myself that coincidences do happen in real life and that this was likely one set of them. If even one fact fails to agree with several others which appear to form a logical pattern, it can't be dismissed and thrown out as merely irrelevant.

It still rained lightly on Saturday morning when I drove over to pick up Seth. The five minutes I waited in the driveway—waited while sitting in my dilapidated pickup truck parked next to a fire-engine red Corvette—seemed an eternity. In that light drizzle, the sight of Seth trudging out with his full backpack and small overnight case only deepened my somber mood. This moment never ceased to sadden me and that dreary morning it was worse than ever. Kids deserve so much better than to be shuttled back and forth between incompatible parents.

Before he got to the truck, Ellen appeared at the front door and, swifter in stride and holding a pair of his boots, approached behind him. I heard her say, "You forgot. You may need these. Don't ruin your good ones."

She opened the passenger door for him and set the boots on the floor of the truck in front of the seat.

As she straightened up, I said I was sincerely sorry for her loss. "I've always felt as close to Harry as to my own father. I'm really sorry to see him go. I'll miss him."

"I know, Mark. Thanks." Hard to tell so perhaps I imagined it, but I sensed genuine sincerity in her tone and downcast eyes.

She stepped to one side, allowing room for Seth, who starred at me in shock while getting into the truck. Those damn bandages again! I quickly made light of it, assuring him I felt fine. "But don't expect me to run a marathon with you or do gymnastics," I warned.

On the road, we eased into the subject of his grandfather's death, agreeing it was good that he was no longer in pain. Seth said he could hardly wait to see if his grandfather would join us the next time we fished at Tyler Pond.

"We won't actually see him, buddy," I said, "but more like it'll be a feeling we have. Maybe we'll think of him when there's a little puff of wind. Or...oh, when a pretty butterfly, say a Monarch butterfly, circles around and rests on the gunnel of the canoe and stays awhile. I'm thinking that's how we'll know he's there."

He wrinkled up his nose and said, "Not a dragonfly, I hope. I don't like those."

"Probably not because he knew how you feel about dragonflies."

"That's good."

All things considered, that weekend wasn't one of our best ones together. Physical activity for me proved limited. I only waded to my knees in the water when the sky had cleared Saturday afternoon and I took Seth to swim at Still-Water Lake, the nearest lake with a good beach. We ate lunch both days at McDonald's. He read some, did his homework and on Sunday watched a couple of films on DVDs he'd brought.

One disappointment for me—instead of his old cell phone he'd brought along a new iPhone, a gift from his mother, he said. Inevitable, but it worried me that in no time he might become as preoccupied with it as Molly was hers. He mentioned the iPhone's source twice, repeating that it was a gift from his mother and not Alan. In fact it came out that Alan hadn't delivered yet on either of his promises of a new iPhone for Molly or a new bike for him. He added the usual comment, saying "I don't need a new bike anyway."

Laughing, I said, "If anybody needs a new bike it would be me. Suppose Alan would buy me one?"

His shook his head vigorously and said, "I don't think so, dad!"

As much as I'd hoped since Tuesday to banish from memory Ellen's harsh criticism of me, her cruel charge that Molly's anxiety was my fault for not having spent more time with the kids, it kept creeping into my consciousness. Seth and I would be doing something together, even simply talking, when out of the blue I'd wonder how I was "rating" at this moment as a dad. I even visualized my effectiveness as it might appear on a meter. Was I doing enough, doing it correctly? A rating of seventy or only forty-five? If I'd screwed up so badly for so many years without realizing it, how could I tell now if I was parenting poorly or well? Seth seemed animated, eyes bright, laughing appropriately, acting normally, or so it seemed. Yet that word Toxic kept haunting me.

I suppose some of my insecurity stemmed from the fact that my own father hadn't provided an ideal role model, not because he didn't love me but because he was so much older than other dad's. I'd calculated it out. He had to have been forty-four when I was born, which meant that he was already fifty-five when I was Seth's age. Which accounted for his not wanting to do many of the physically active things which dad's often do with their kids, especially their sons.

One aspect of it which cheered me a bit was that at least he called me Dad. That probably didn't mean anything but I'd always hated hearing Ellen address her father as Harry. Blanche was Mom but her father was Harry, apparently from the beginning and all through her childhood. I'd struggled with it in silence. I know some modern, so-called progressive parents foster the custom but given that in most respects Blanche and Harry where a traditional couple I couldn't help but view Ellen's use of his first name as a symbol of disrespect toward her father. A telling sign of disaffection? Perhaps only of indifference.

Before the weekend was out I remembered to casually mention the spare key to my apartment. "Just curious," I said, "but where do you keep the spare key, Seth. The one to the door here?"

He frowned. "In my room, hanging on a nail. Why?"

"Oh, no reason. Just wondering. So it's safe."

"Yes. It's by my bed."

"Sounds good. Is it, ah…labeled in some way? Have my name on it, for instance?"

"Yeah dad, why?"

"Oh, just wondering. bud. I'm always finding keys lying around and forgetting what they go to, that's all."

He shrugged and said, "I don't. I'll remember."

That next week things began settling back to normal for me. On Monday I kept a follow-up appointment with the doctor who'd treated me the week before. He took off the bandages and said I was healing nicely. He told me—which I already knew—that I'd likely experience some pain in my left ribs "for several weeks to come." Wonderful. I've never been one to spend a lot of time admiring my face in a mirror. A good thing— when I returned to my apartment and did take a look, my face wasn't a pleasant sight. At least my eyes weren't still blood-shot as they'd been for so many days after the accident.

I covered a couple of meetings that week and did a human inter-est feature story for Al; also sold some ads for him on Wednesday.

On Tuesday and again on Wednesday afternoon I happened to drive past Alan Ames' used car lot out on Route Two; just happened to count the vehicles lined up at an angle next to the road. Each day there were only five, including one pickup truck, a Blue Toyota Tacoma.

On Thursday night I got a phone call from Dottie. After initial greetings she told me she had an appointment in Collinsville at ten-thirty the next morning.

"I'm wondering if you'll be free for lunch?" she asked.

"Sure." Why not, I hadn't yet maxed out my credit card.

"This appointment shouldn't take much over an hour so I can probably meet you right at twelve," she said.

"Sounds good."

We agreed to meet at the little family-style restaurant on Main Street.

After the call, I was left wondering what she wanted to talk with me about. She hadn't given me a clue. That's the problem, I thought, when people don't provide enough information. When they leave blanks, someone like me tries filling them in with his own imagination.

Dottie arrived at the restaurant promptly at noon: tall, gray-haired, confident in bearing, dressed in a simple, no-nonsense green and beige plaid work shirt and brown cargo pants. In a somewhat incongruent mix of images, she carried a fancy, brown leather brief case.

"Actually, Mark, I've made two stops over here this morning," she said as we sat at a table. "Should have called ahead probably, but I took a chance and stopped by the funeral home. As luck would have it there was somebody there who could give me Harry's ashes."

The waiter appeared and took our order. Dottie told him she would be paying the tab—told him in so firm a tone that I knew any protest was futile.

After we'd given our orders she picked up where she'd left off, saying, "Anyway, Harry left specific instructions that they be divided in half. One container to be buried next to Blanche and the other half he wanted spread on the water at...I'd have to check again but I think it said Tyler Pond." Her inflection made it a question.

"Yes, I'm sure. Perfect!" I didn't intentionally shout.

She blinked.

"It was Harry's favorite place for getting away," I explained, lowering my voice. "That and It fits in with what Seth and I talked about over the weekend. He loved his Grandpa Harry, you know. So I told him Harry's spirit would likely be at Tyler Pond the next time we fished there."

"I see what you mean. So how did the kids take it?" she asked.

"I can't say how Molly did because I haven't seen Molly. Going on almost two months now. I think Seth's doing okay. He understands that it's for the best that Harry isn't still suffering."

She nodded. "Kids usually have it together better than some adults."

Remembering my reaction to hearing Dottie's news a week earlier, I had to agree.

"Would you mind doing that part of it for me?" she asked. "I suppose they should be spread on the water well out from shore. I'm not much for being on boats."

I said, "I want to, Dottie. It would be an honor. Thanks for asking."

"There's no hurry. I have the box in my car."

"No ceremony? None at all?"

She shook her head. "No. He was most insistent on that."

"It would be a huge one, Dottie. Everybody in this community thought the world of Harry. There wouldn't be a church or auditorium big enough to hold all the people here who'd come."

"I'm sure you're right, and that's what he wanted to avoid. All the fuss of a large funeral. He put it very clearly in writing and I remember his telling me right after Blanche's funeral he didn't want anything like that done for him. No hocus-pocus, as he put it. I'm trying to follow what he wanted to the letter, at least as much as possible."

"Sure. Back to the ashes...what a nice touch," I said, appreciating the irony. "Blanche still gets half."

She allowed herself a restrained smile. "Yes," she said, "Blanche still gets half. The funeral home will arrange for that so I have only the one box. I really appreciate you're doing that, Mark. Anyway," she continued, a bit brusquely, "I've just been at the lawyer's office, at Hardy and Danforth's, and picked up everything I'll need to start settling Harry's estate. The will does have to be probated. I didn't know that when we spoke last night. But nearly all the assets are in both your names already so those are pretty straightforward. On those, all I need to do is file the paperwork for each account and return it with copies of the death certificate."

"Both names? Whose names?"

"Yours and Harry's. On most of his assets. Including the house."

I sat staring at her in stunned silence.

"I'd wondered if Harry ever told you what he planned." She paused, searching my face. "I guess maybe he didn't. It's true, Mark, the bulk of Harry's estate is to go to you. Including the house. Harry didn't put any restrictions on anything either. Nothing in trust, for example, but naturally he was thinking in terms of your caring for the kids. Eduction and so forth."

"I don't know what to say, Dottie. No, I...I had no...I mean no idea whatsoever. None." My throat had gone dry. "I've, well, I've just always assumed that Harry's whole estate would go to Ellen."

Smiling, she said, drolly, "Without a doubt, so did she."

"You mean she won't get—"

"Oh, she'll get some. He hasn't cut her out entirely. And there is the stipulation that if you should die before the kids come of age, the remaining assets revert to Ellen. I think that's a standard clause. But anyway, you'll be getting the bulk of it. As his power of attorney, they send me all the quarterly and annual investment statements. The last time I added the accounts with your name on them as co-owner, they totaled over a million eight. I haven't gone through all the latest statements so the final figure will be higher. As far as the house goes, it's rented right now but not on a long term lease. I'll handle that part of it with the realtor so they can give notice to the tenants. I'll keep you posted on that."

"Dottie I can't...can't get over it. That...that Harry had that much money in assets for one thing. I mean, almost two million?"

"As you know, he worked hard. That was a big business he built up over the years. It's true Blanche cost him a small fortune every time he turned around, but as long as he kept her happy, she never cared or knew the full extent of the money coming in or that he'd put away. He paid for good investment advice and over the years simply socked away the extra money without telling her. Mostly in an annuity and three or four bond funds. I expect a good deal of it came from selling the business too, when he did. He never told me exactly what he got for it but I'm sure it netted him a good amount of money."

"But..." I was still reeling in shock, "... why?"

"Why what? Why didn't he leave it all to Ellen?"

"Well, yes."

"Partly because he knew she wouldn't manage the money as wisely as you would. And also because he felt you got a raw deal when you and Ellen divorced. He confided in me at the time. Said he hoped you'd be awarded joint custody of the kids and stay in the house you worked so hard to rebuild. When it didn't turn out that way he felt terrible for you. In fact it was right after your divorce settlement that he did a transfer deed on the house, listing you as co-owner."

"But I'm, well, I'm not even still family. Ellen's his own daughter and yet..."

"Naturally, he loved Ellen," she said, "He hasn't cut her out entirely, of course. But he loved and respected you as a son-in-law and he knew you'd handle the financial arrangement for the kids better than she would. To a large extent I guess you could call it a practical matter. Not strictly that but partly that, yes."

"I'm speechless," I said. "Just didn't expect it and still can't believe it." I paused for a moment and then went on, "So when did you know?"

"Know how he'd divide his assets up?"

I nodded.

"He confided in me from time to time so I knew how he was thinking. I'd say his mind was mostly made up after he'd heard the terms of your divorce. He told me then that he'd try to even things up."

"So..." I was thinking back to that last time we were with Harry, "...was this what you were thinking of when Harry tried to speak, I mean after he saw my bandages? That he was so upset over seeing me injured like that, knowing how he'd left things?"

"Yes," she said, nodding. "I wasn't absolutely sure then whether he'd followed through. I've known of people swearing they'll cut a family member out of their wills and then when push comes to shove, blood is thicker, as they say. It's too drastic. They can't go ahead with it. Knowing Harry, I figured he would and he did."

"Well, I certainly never knew."

"As I said over the phone last week, Harry was one of the finest men I've ever known." Just as the server approached our table, balancing a loaded tray near his shoulder, she lowered her voice and said, "I'll tell one thing, Mark. I'm trying real hard not to hold it against Harry that he didn't will it all to me for my dog shelter."

# 19

HARDY AND DANFORTH, the legal firm whose office was located next to the hardware store. Hardy and Danforth, the firm which held Harry's written will and had presumably done his legal work. Hardy and Danforth...the name lodged somewhere in my subconsciousness.

It took most of Thursday afternoon to adjust to Dottie's bombshell, the totally unexpected news that I was to inherit nearly two million dollars and my late in-laws' house. I had known that Harry was fond of me. I'd always felt the strong bond between us, both of us tradesmen and both married to strong-willed women whose greatest enjoyment in life often seemed to derive from spending money. After our divorce, however, I'd never imagined that Harry would favor me over his daughter in drawing up his will. He loved the kids but he'd certainly known that Ellen had been awarded custody of them.

Hardy and Danforth. Bit by bit my memory produced a match until I finally remembered the context of where and from whom I'd most recently heard mention of the legal firm. The earliest reference had come when Ralph and I had met that first time while riding our bikes and had spoken of our respective families. He'd said Alan Ames' sister worked for Hardy and Danforth. That was it, of course! And then much later, that Saturday night over beer at the bar with Todd and Ben, the subject had come up again. They'd mentioned that Alan Ames' sister, the one whose husband had been killed while serving in the military, worked for Hardy and Danforth.

I slept poorly that night. Harry's will. A possible motive for Adam Ames to kill me. Molly's anxiety/depression. Todd's prospects for getting the condo contract. Maggie's suggestion that I should buy the Collinsville Banner. My thoughts swirled together in an unmanageable stew. Experts now say that multi-tasking is actually impossible, that we humans cannot focus our full attention on more than one task of any complexity at a time. The belief that we can does seem to break down when we analyze how well we've accomplished the multiple tasks we claim to have done simultaneously. The principle probably applies to our thought process as well. For me, the effect of all these muddled thoughts was major sleeplessness.

In the midst of confusion, life still had to go on. Friday was launder mat day—two hours of potentially numbing boredom unless I either ran into someone interesting to talk with or went armed with a magazine. I stopped at the drug store on my way there and bought a **Time** magazine. It turned out the only other patron was an elderly woman, just then folding her clothes. By the time I'd filled my two washing machines, she'd left, leaving me in solitude to read—or, attempt to as stray thoughts kept diverting me from the page. Little by little I was making progress in sorting out my troublesome issues, putting frames around them and arranging them in manageable order.

Dottie had delivered great news but I saw that being named as heir to nearly two million dollars wasn't the same as winning a lottery. Harry hadn't intended the money for my use but for the kids'. What if either or both decided to become professionals, doctors or lawyers for example? Four, six, even eight years of education could easily top a half a million dollars in expense, probably more given the inflation rate increases by the time Seth got there. Harry's wealth wasn't intended for my use directly but for me to administer in stewardship for the kids' benefit and that was fine with me. I'd never wanted to be wealthy. But I could use some of it and it would be there as a cushion. I wouldn't need to worry any longer over how to pay my bills until I was back to work.

And Harry's gift of the house, what a godsend! That part seemed especially surreal. A mortgage-free house! It was far larger and fancier than I needed or wanted—I'd have to adjust to Blanche's pretentious excesses—but the house was something I could call my own with a clear conscience. I had personally done much of the remodeling work on it; I had also been forced to give up any claim on the one house I might have been entitled to.

Another matter which I reflected long and hard on was the Collinsville Banner. Tempted though I was to explore Maggie's suggestion further, to broach the subject of buying it with Al, I knew deep down that I wasn't temperamentally well-suited to owning and operating a weekly newspaper. Sure, I could do it and even become successful but would I be happy doing it? The answer was an unequivocal no.

That evening I got a phone call from Todd. I could tell by the upbeat tone of voice that it was good news.

"They've accepted my bid," he said. "Got a confirmation letter in the mail today. I've just been on the phone lining up the site work. Assuming the foundation gets poured on schedule we should be able to start work the second or third week in October. Thought you'd appreciate hearing."

"Damn, Todd, nice going! I guess to hell I appreciate hearing! I can't wait. Ought to be in pretty good shape by then, too," I said. "Nothing wrong with my right arm. Probably won't be into a lot of lifting for a while but other than that...wow! Great news! Can't wait!"

We shot the bull for a couple of more minutes and then, as the conversation wound down, Todd suddenly said, "Oh yeah, I almost forgot. Ben said to tell you he went by that used car lot this afternoon, Ellen's boyfriend's place?"

"Yeah?"

"Said the F-150 is back out there parked next to the Tacoma."

"Really. Very interesting. Thanks, Todd, and please thank Ben for me. Guess I may just take a run out there myself and have a look. Maybe early tomorrow morning."

"The other thing he said was not to buy it because it's a piece of crap."

"Yeah, he mentioned that before. I'm wondering if it's in even worse shape now," I said, "maybe with a patched up fender."

That night I prepared. I entered Chief Clem McDonald's cell, office and home phone numbers into my cell phone, and also the number Sgt. Waterman had given me. I made sure both my phone and camera were charging so as to be full by morning.

Thinking ahead to the morning, I dreaded going to Mr. Ames' used car lot but could see no other way around it. My theory of what had happened was only that, a theory. My hunch could be wrong. Asking Clem or State Trooper Waterman to check out a pickup truck merely on the strength of a suspicion of mine would be foolish. Possibly a waste of their time and likely adding a blemish to my credibility. No, I had to check out the truck myself first.

It stood to reason that Alan Ames would be open for business on Saturday but I had no idea when he normally opened. I assumed perhaps at eight, which meant that if I got there at seven-fifteen I should have plenty of time to take a thorough look at the truck. Seeing my own truck, his sister might call him but I knew it would take ten minutes for him to get there.

Saturday morning dawned partly sunny with a nippy chill in the air. I put on a light jacket before leaving. The leaves on the maples outside my apartment were starting to turn color, beautiful splotches here and there of red and orange among the shades of green; I saw a good amount of early color along Route Two also, more tending toward gold and even a mixing in of browns on hardwoods nearest the road.

I parked just off the main highway on the car-lot side of the drive, removed my camera from the case, slid my cell phone into a pocket and got out. Heavy dew had wetted the unkempt grass in front of the row of used vehicles, enough that it felt slippery underfoot as I walked along toward the two pickup trucks parked at the end.

Within seconds of passing by the Toyota I saw what I was there to find. Anyone not looking for it could have missed the waviness in the wide bumper assembly where it rounded to the left side and ended in front of the tire but I spotted it and, drawing closer, easily felt it with my fingers. There had been some filling in with body filler and the left section, over to about the middle, clearly had been repainted, as evidenced by a tapering-off effect and differences in paint shading and texture. I bent down and sniffed. It smelled of new lacquer.

The split headlamp lens—clear glass for the road light and smaller amber lens rounding to the side—appeared new, sparkling brighter in the sunlight than the matching lens on the right. The fender panel itself, when I sighted along it into the light, was unblemished but a shinier black than either the hood or door panel adjacent to it. Sniffing at it confirmed that it also had very recently been painted. Without especially searching I even noticed two tell-tale paint runs, proof if any were needed, that Mr. Ames was a rank amateur at spay painting.

Stepping back from the truck, I imagined how I must have been struck. Less damage to the front and to the bumper itself suggested that my rear wheel had easily crumpled, that it was the bike seat which had smashed the headlight and had grazed and dented the fender panel so badly he'd had to replace it. I had been struck by the corner, which threw me off to the side and out of the way. In other words, it could have been much worse.

I wasted no time calling Clem, luckily finding him at his office on the first try. It took more than a couple of minutes to make him understand what I was saying, what I wanted him to do. He said he'd be there as soon as he could. (I imagined him leisurely finishing his coffee, maybe reading the rest of the sports page in the Collinsville Record, and then, taking his own sweet time, moseying along out to his cruiser.) I put the phone in my pocket and took several pictures with the camera, from the side, the front, and close-ups from more than one angle. I knelt down and snapped shots of the tire tread on the front tires, then got up and went to the back and took shots of a rear tire. Perhaps an unnecessary precaution but I wasn't risking any chance of the truck coming up missing again.

Just as I finished I heard a vehicle with a loud muffler coming along the road. It slowed and turned in. The red Corvette. It proceeded on up the driveway as I walked back to my truck, put the camera back in its case and set it on the seat. I closed the door and stood next to the truck as he walked at an eager pace down the driveway. About my height and build, maybe a few pounds heavier.

"Give you a great deal on it," he called out from ten yards or so away. Approaching closer and holding out his hand, he said, "Time to trade up, is it? Hi, I'm Alan..." a flicker of recognition. Maybe Ellen hadn't destroyed all our wedding pictures?

"Mark Sloan," I said, shaking his hand.

I'd never seen the charm in anyone's face drain as quickly as it did from the face of Mr. Ames, in his case replaced by hostility. It probably was, as Maggie had said, a very handsome face. Handsome male faces don't do anything for me so I can't vouch for it. One thing was for certain, however: Alan Ames was not happy to see me. An awkward moment to say the least, for both of us.

"I'm not here to buy, Mr. Ames," I said, steadying my voice, "I'm here to check out that Ford-150 on the end. Looks like it's run into something and been repaired. Very recently."

He glared. "I don't know what you're talking about."

"I think you do. I think you know exactly what I'm talking about. Why did you do it, Alan? Why did you run me over?"

We stared at one another, face to face only two feet apart. In my peripheral vision I saw his right hand clench in a fist. I was as mentally prepared as I could be but twinges of pain in my left side reminded me of my physical vulnerabilities. I was in no shape to fight.

"You're crazy. Get off my land!" His eyes suddenly blazed with anger.

"I want the whole story. Now, Mr. Ames."

"Bastard! Off my land!" The distended veins in his temple pulsed with purple in the morning sun.

Three seconds of stalemate, then hellish fury...

A reflexive twist barely spared my left flank from his brutal first punch to my gut, centering it, merely winding me. I gasped for air, lunged forward and delivered a swift, solid right punch to his stomach, knocking him down onto the wet grass. On the recoil, pain shot protestingly though my left side.

As he sprang up—panting, eyes wide in savage rage—every nerve and muscle in me quivered with adrenaline but every instinct warned of danger. Normally an easy match for an Alan Ames, I was far from normal.

He paused for a moment on his feet, muttered a coarse obscenity, calling me an "eff-ing son-of-a-bitch," then came at me quickly, with a fist jab aimed again at my vulnerable left side.

I dodged, narrowly parrying the blow but was momentarily thrown off balance. Seizing the opportunity, he moved in swiftly with another punch to my left rib cage, this time succeeding.

Pain, excruciating, nerve shattering pain—the worst I'd ever felt—instantly racked the whole left side of my body. I staggered back, caught my balance again, desperately fought the impulse to double over in agony and drop.

He muttered another vulgar expletive, jerked toward me, but then paused unexpectedly, distracted—I would learn a minute later—by Clem McDonald's police cruiser. In his three seconds of inattentiveness, with my back to the road and not yet seeing Clem, I summoned the strength—fueled I'm sure by near-murderous vengefulness—to deliver one final, bare-knuckled right punch, this one to the unguarded jaw of his pretty face. It sent him sprawling to the ground. (And that afternoon, I understand, to a surgeon who wired the shattered bones together.)

# 20

THE LEAVES CONTINUED their annual cycle, growing more and more colorful, painting the hills surrounding Collinsville in vivd reds, oranges and golds, and then one by one falling, rendering the naked limbs defenseless against the increasingly cold winds of November. We've already gotten a first, very light dusting of snow which melted as soon as it hit the ground. A mere prelude to what will follow as winter closes in.

Todd, Ben and I are making good progress on the condominiums. Todd hired a fellow named Josh to work during the first three weeks while I was recuperating but apparently Josh wasn't much of a carpenter. I didn't meet him—Todd hired him with the understanding the job was only temporary and let him go the Friday before I got back to work. (They still occasionally regale me with Joshisms.) My ribs will continue to be sore for some time but each day I'm gaining strength. Against all odds, neither Alan Ames' truck nor his fist struck my rib cage with force enough to puncture my lung. The doctor—the same one I'd had following my earlier biking accident, a man taciturn until then—turned unexpectedly loquacious the day he released me from the hospital that second time, saying that if I had a death wish, which he suspected I did, then a third episode should be the charm!

Ellen hasn't let me know how well Molly is progressing, whether or not the counseling is helping. No big surprise there. I did speak with Molly on the phone when Seth called to wish me a happy birthday. After telling me he had a special present he'd give me that next Saturday, he put her on, apparently at her request. She also said she hoped I was having a nice birthday, then asked about the cuts on my face. Had they healed yet? As Ellen wasn't there when they called, I assume Molly acted of her own volition.

Seth's birthday gift turned out to be a watercolor painting he'd done, a nice view of Tyler Pond from our canoe. Near the bottom of the scene, he'd painted in a butterfly, perched on the gunnel.

"Grandpa Harry?" I asked.

He nodded. "Yup."

"Is this another butterfly in the air over here?" It was black, however, not bright orange.

"Uh, uh, dad. Can't you tell? It's a dragonfly."

"Oh yes, so it is. Very good. I love the painting, Seth." If he were a few years older I might have quipped that the dragonfly could be his Grandmother Blanche.

Although the phone call was the only contact I've had with Molly, reference was made to her at work a couple of days ago by Ben in connection with his brother. It seems that Brian—"my little shithead brother," in Ben's colorful narrative—is now a sophomore in high school and it seems that Brian recently asked Molly to a school dance. Neither Brian nor Molly has a license yet and as Todd begged off from transporting them to and from the dance, older brother Ben got stuck with the chore.

To hear him tell it they must have made a striking couple. "So she was wearing this long white dress," he said, "with the neck coming way down here..." with his finger he traced a deep V shape down nearly to his navel, "and these long slits up the outside of both legs." Yup, that be my daughter Molly, I thought: mod, chic, learning well at the feet of her mother. "So here's numb-nuts, comes out in his droopy jeans, crotch hanging down to here..." again a gesture half-way to his knees, "and his greasy Sox cap."

"Backward? The cap?"

"Course."

"Impressive," I said.

"Then she starts—oh, your name came up, dude."

"It did, huh?"

"Yeah, but not till on the way back from the gym. She starts dissing you. Going to me like, 'Must be fun working with my faaather'. She gets this real sick look. Like she's gonna puke. I won't say what she called you."

"Thanks, Ben, for sparing me that much. I can imagine, though."

"No fear, man, I got your back. I let her have it but good. Said she didn't know shit. Told her you do twice the work my old man does. 'If it wasn't for your pop,' I said, 'mine would a gone under years ago.' You'd a been proud, dude."

"Hey, thanks, Ben. Not true, but I really appreciate it. That must have gone over big with Molly."

He'd nodded. "She turned pretty quiet rest of the way home."

Sad to admit that I took some comfort when listening to Ben's account. It's hardly a breakthrough. But hearing someone else's positive opinion of me can't hurt, especially if the someone isn't that much older. Maybe if Molly and Todd's brother continue to...no, scratch that. Not likely unless little Brian cleans up his act. The baseball cap alone would be a deal breaker with Molly!

Blanche and Harry's house is still occupied by renters, which is okay. Dottie says the realtors have given them notice and it should be vacant by the end of December. Naturally, I'm thrilled, yet in all honesty, the house isn't really "Me." Ironic that my benefactor, Harry, was also the one person who had best modeled minimalism for me, something I would find difficult taking to extremes in my own life but something to strive for in a world seemingly gone mad with excess. The house is way bigger than I need now, or will need, even if I'm successful in gaining custody of Seth. (I filed the paperwork last week to begin that process.) Blanche's walk-in closet is larger than the bedroom in my apartment. That house is also filled with memories, some good, some not so good. I guess one of the big pluses is the huge basement where I can set up the well-equipped workshop I've always wanted. At the moment my tools are divided between the contractor's chest on the back of the pickup and several boxes on the floor of my one tiny closet.

I'm back to covering one or two evening meeting a week for Al, also feature stories as they come along, fitting it all in between my regular work. Al and Maggie are planning a two-week European river cruise vacation together In May provided he can line up reliable help to get out two issues of the paper in their absence. I've volunteered to do as much as I can but made it clear I can't become an interim editor due to my full- time carpentry job. (And to think I was desperate, without any job at all for a period during the past summer.)

Little Don Dornier and his partners have won approval from the Public Service Board to build a test tower on the mountain. (Regrettably, I wasn't able to come up with a convincing connection, financial or even social between him and any Board member as I'd hoped. Water over the dam now.) It doesn't take a crystal ball to predict that within three years' time a line of behemoth wind generators will mar the formerly scenic mountain ridge, producing unnecessary power but boosting Vermont's bragging rights as the Greenest Energy State in the union.

Little Don's brother, Roger, took out a full page ad in the Banner two weeks ago announcing a gun sale to "End All Gun Sales." For three days last week the volume of vehicular traffic on that side of the village dwarfed that of any previous event ever held in the history Collinsville. Traffic backed up so badly the first day that Roger was forced to hire one of Clem's deputies to direct the flow and manage parking. Testosterone-charged rednecks—not all male, either—descended on Collinsville, some from neighboring states and even from Quebec, Canada. Every fourth or fifth pickup, by my count the one time I drove through, sported either an American or Confederate flag.

And as far as Alan Ames, what will happen is anybody's guess at this point. He was arraigned on charges of leaving the scene of an accident, made bail, and is currently awaiting trial. I've heard that a public defender has taken his case and that in spite of the overwhelming evidence it was his Ford F-150 which struck me on Verge Road, he is pleading not guilty. The evidence includes tire tread marks matching his truck tires, a newly-replaced and painted fender (the investigator even found the original crumpled one on a metal heap behind the house), and an exact paint match with paint found on my bike frame.

All I'm seeking is coverage of my medical expenses. Nothing to be gained by asking for an additional half million or so in pain and suffering when the guy apparently doesn't have two nickels to rub together.

One potentially complicating factor was Ames' threat to press assault charges against me for breaking his jaw in our fist-swinging altercation. He'd shouted it as Clem was taking over the scene on Saturday. Luckily for me, the Chief ignored it, focusing instead on subduing Ames then calling for backup. I remember saying, "He threw the first punch" to Clem and I think he took it at face value. If Ames tried the idea out later, say with his lawyer, I'm guessing it was squashed at least partly because of his prior criminal record. I'd like to think my own credibility and standing as a citizen in the community also played into it.

What's missing here, of course, are some additional details which could radically alter the charges against Alan Ames if they were explored. The assumption apparently being made is that Mr. Ames was distracted while driving and struck me accidentally. I, on the other hand, firmly believe he intended to kill me, that he made the attempt and failed a total of four times. I think his sister, who works as a secretary for Hardy and Danforth, had knowledge of Harry's will and the accompanying documentation in his file which listed his assets, and that she shared that information with her brother. I'm only guessing but would suppose he took up with Ellen first, thinking she'd soon be inheriting a good bit of money and a house, only to then learn from his sister that she wouldn't. Wouldn't, that is, unless her ex-husband were eliminated.

I debated long and hard over whether to connect those dots for the police and in the end decided against it. I asked myself what purpose would be served and concluded the answer was none. His sister could deny having knowledge of Harry's estate; if it were proven she had access to it she could deny having shared any information with her brother. He would back her up, deny any knowledge and maintain his innocence of anything beyond having accidentally struck me.

And even if it were proven that he acted intentionally on that strong motive to kill me and was convicted of attempted murder, I doubted our lenient judicial system in Vermont would mete out a significant punishment. And even if did, our state allows for a seemingly endless series of appeals and delays that can take years to resolve. Justice here is often a long, drawn out affair.

I hated the thought of a woman on the staff at Hardy and Danforth getting away with such an egregious breach of confidentiality, escaping firing from her job at the very least. I hated the idea of Alan Ames merely facing charges of negligent driving with accident resulting and leaving the scene. But I think there's more to be said for walking away from some wrongs. Not forgiving or forgetting them, just putting them to rest.

All things are relative and the biggest positive here, the best part of the whole stinking situation, is that Ellen kicked Ames out of her house the day after she read about the hit and run charges against him in the Collinsville Record. The news article revealed that Ames has a prior criminal record and had served three years of a five year prison sentence in Michigan on a range of charges including auto theft and robbery. I'll settle for that much, a profound feeling of gratitude that he's no longer living in Ellen's household, influencing our kids.

One big question remaining is whether Ellen knew of Alan's plan. I'd rather believe she didn't. Leading up to our separation and divorce and for several months thereafter, Ellen disliked me with a passion. I don't believe, however, that at any time she's felt strongly enough to wish for my death. Certainly it isn't consistent with what I know of her character and I don't believe she conspired with Alan. She likes money, for sure, but not to the extent of aiding in a murder to get it.

Yesterday afternoon I carried a small box out to the pickup, loaded the canoe in the back, and drove out to Tyler Pond.

It was chilly, the air still, the clear water calm, the cloudless sky a deep blue. Except for a few yellow hold-outs, the leaves on all the trees along the shore had fallen. I shivered as I shoved the canoe into the water and stepped in to take up the paddle.

I dispersed the ashes toward the middle, my solemn act witnessed by a late-passing, southward-bound flock of Canada geese.

45123913R00102

Made in the USA
Middletown, DE
24 June 2017